FIFTY PACES FORWARD!

Colin Saunders

FOOTLINE PRESS

First edition 2020

© Footline Press 2020

Text copyright © Colin Saunders 2020

Photographs copyright © 2020:
Front cover Michael Kohn
Inside front cover David Lewis
Inside back cover Bob Goodman

ISBN 978 0 9929434 3 1

The author is especially grateful to Fiona Barltrop and Stuart Walker for proofreading, and to the following for other help and encouragement with producing this book: Bob Goodman, Patricia Edwards, Lucy Hall at Lucy's Web Designs, Dr Alan Harrington, Inuit Art Foundation, Michael Kohn, David Lewis and Visit Greenland, as well as many members of the Long Distance Walkers Association, The Ramblers and the Vanguards Rambling Club.

Published by Footline Press
35 Gerrards Close, London, N14 4RH.

Printed by Inky Little Fingers Ltd.
Churcham, Gloucester, GL2 8AX.

CONTENTS

Before you read on, the author would like to say a few words:

Thank you for choosing to read this book, I hope you'll enjoy it. The story is set in the early 1960s, and the title comes from a traditional command at the time (though maybe not used so much these days) to the gentlemen in a party of ramblers to walk ahead and allow the ladies to relieve themselves in the bushes, without fear of being discovered by a person or persons of the opposite gender.

I started walking regularly for pleasure in 1967, on the magnificent and much missed weekly ramblers excursions of that period, which attracted hundreds of people. Their true story is told in my book, *Rambling away from 'The Smoke'* (Footline Press, 2014), though it is now out of print.

It was on these excursions that the Vanguards Rambling Club was established (the name comes from having to sit in the guard's van on the homeward train!) and I have had the enormous pleasure of being a member since 1967. I was also a leader on many of those excursions. The club has since gone on to create the Vanguard Way, a 66-mile trail from Croydon to the Sussex coast – details at vanguardway.org.uk.

We had such a wonderful time on the excursions, enjoying good company, beautiful countryside, stops for lunch at a pub, afternoon tea at a café, and sometimes another pub before boarding the homeward train. And with many young people present, romances blossomed, and many of them resulted in marriages and families.

The success of these excursions resulted in very large numbers of people walking together, sometimes a hundred or more in one group. This was difficult to manage and some leaders got fed up with it, so set up their own excursions, with mixed fortunes.

In this book, I have imagined the adventures and misadventures of one such offshoot. Some are based on things that really happened, which I have developed a little... or maybe a lot! So I should make plain that all the characters and situations in this book are fictitious, and any resemblance to real people is purely coincidental.

Some explanations are due to ramblers (hikers, walkers etc) who may be reading this book. On those excursions, what are nowadays referred to as 'backmarkers' were called 'rearguards', while 'recces' (reconnaissances) were 'surveys'.

Leaders were expected to carry out a survey beforehand, to check the paths, pubs and tea places, then report any problems so that they could be sorted in time for the actual day.

Programmes of the excursions were published for each season, showing destinations, times and fares. A mock programme relevant to this story is included in Chapter 2 of Part One. And if you think, 'Hang on, they're walking in the opposite direction to the advertised schedule,' well, that's what happened sometimes – it was up to the leaders to decide which way to go.

Some readers may try to follow the stories on a map, but it would be futile. Whilst most of the railway stations I have referred to are genuine, to give an approximate idea of location, most of the places in between are imaginary. And don't go checking the weather records either! They have been invented to suit the story.

Of course, the action takes place well before the invention of mobile phones, satellite navigation and other aspects of modern life. For example, if someone got lost, or needed to contact somebody else, they just had to make the best of it or wait until they found a telephone.

Finally, I would like to thank the many friends I have made during my walking 'career'. Without their inspiration and encouragement, writing this story would have been unthinkable and impossible.

Colin Saunders
September 2020

PART 1

FIFTY PACES FORWARD!

CHAPTER 1

PROLOGUE

Sunday 29th October, 1961
The Devil's Punchbowl, Surrey

Sorry if this offends anyone, but there can be no denying that, figuratively speaking, Dan Rose was finally pushed into action by Tsubrina's ample bosom.

Dan was one of the regular leaders on the ramblers' excursions from London. One warm autumn Sunday, he was leading one of the six parties on an excursion by train from Waterloo to Witley and Haslemere, to explore the glorious countryside on the Hampshire/ Surrey border.

Some six hundred ramblers were on the train. Most had alighted at Witley to form four parties – Party Numbers One, Two, Three and Four. But Dan (leading Party Number Five) and another leader, Alf Trayton (leading Party Number Six) had continued to Haslemere, with about two hundred ramblers split between them.

It was rather warm for October. After a somewhat lengthy pub lunch stop in Hindhead, the members of Party Number Five were in a relaxed mood, admiring the autumnal leaves that glittered as they danced in and out of the sunshine – a kaleidoscope of brown, red, orange and yellow.

With Dan in the lead, they descended into the Devil's Punch Bowl, a vast, wooded depression in the far south-western corner of Surrey.

On reaching the foot of the bowl, Dan stopped and waited for his party to catch up. He almost blended into the background. A retired army officer in his late sixties, he was fit, stocky, muscular and tanned, wearing lightweight, brown military fatigues and a dark green bucket hat that hid his totally bald scalp. At a quick glance, in the shade, he might have been mistaken for a mature tree.

Close behind Dan came two young women. Rosalyn Kemp was slim and pretty, mid-twenties, with shoulder-length light brown hair, wearing a navy blue shirt and black knee-length breeches with long, dark green socks. Her spectacles made her look intelligent – which she was, being an actuarial trainee in the City of London.

Rosalyn's friend, Winifred Biddles, of similar age, was rather plain, a little on the plump side, with a shock of red curly hair, dressed in a brown sweater and knee-length grey skirt. A pair of short grey socks revealed her well-developed calf muscles.

After several minutes, Dan said, "Where've they got to?" and shouted, "Hallo!" There was no reply. He tried again, with the same result.

Taking off his rucksack, he opened a side pocket and took out a whistle. Blowing a whistle was supposed to let people know where the leader was. He blew it with such force that the trilling of a nearby blackbird turned to angry squawks as it flew away. A grey squirrel, which had been idly observing the proceedings from a nearby beech tree, fell off its perch, clattered down several lower branches, eventually grabbed hold of one and scrambled back up. But there was no human response.

Dan thumped the undergrowth beside the path with his walking stick. They had been waiting for a good five minutes now, and he was not happy.

"Where *have* they got to?" he repeated. He studied his map, contained in a map-case slung around his neck. "They were right behind me when we crossed that junction, and there's been no other turning since."

"Maybe someone had an accident and they're helping them," said Winifred.

Dan considered the idea. "Don't think so. Someone would've come on to let me know."

Rosalyn said, "I'll go back and see what's happened". But before she could set off, a tall, gangling, middle-aged, sad-looking man shambled into view.

"Aha!" exclaimed Dan. "Here's Percy, at least."

Percival Fordingbridge wore the jacket of what had once been a pin-striped suit, and a khaki nether garment, which drooped to a point at which it was difficult to tell whether they were shorts or knee breeches. His hair was a straggly brown and he wore thick, horn-rimmed glasses. Although much the same age, he did not compare well to Dan, being round-shouldered with a slight stoop, and looking like he'd topple over if you blew in his ear.

"Are the others with you, Percy?" asked Dan.

"No." boomed Percy. Belying his stature, his voice was full of vigour, a rich *basso profundo* that seemed to echo round the Punch Bowl.

"I crossed that junction quite close behind you," he continued. "Then I heard a great babble and stopped to see what it was, and Alf Trayton's party came round a corner. He ignored us and marched across, cutting off the rest of our lot. So I waited, and by the time they had passed, our lot had all but disappeared. I reckon they must have thought his lot was our lot, and tagged on behind."

"Whaaat!" spluttered Dan. "Alf's a fool. Seeing us crossing, he should have held up his party until we'd passed. Couldn't you have called them back?"

"I did," replied Percy, "but they took no notice then disappeared around a bend."

"Well, he must have an enormous party now," observed Rosalyn.

Dan groaned. "There were seventy-six of us, less us four, that leaves seventy-two. I'd say Alf originally had about a hundred and twenty, so now he's leading a booted army of almost two hundred." He started whacking a patch of stinging nettles with his stick. "Gah!" he yelled, for effect.

"Have you been stung by those nettles, Dan?" asked Winnie.

Dan ignored her. "And even my son, Ollie, must have gone the wrong way too."

Percy said. "Yes, I did see Ollie, actually. He was talking to that young woman who's Alf's rearguard."

"Tsubrina!" exclaimed Rosalyn.

Dan exploded. "Damn and blast it! Ollie's my rearguard. We surveyed the route last weekend, so he should know it." He whacked a nearby tree several times with his stick, then began beating some bracken to a pulp.

Rosalyn eyed him with concern. "Steady on Dan, this isn't like you at all."

Dan looked at her and half-smiled. "Sorry, Ros, but I've just about had enough of the Great White Hunter and these huge parties."

The 'Great White Hunter' was Dunsinane Goblick, the overweight and overbearing organiser of the ramblers' excursions. The soubriquet resulted from his tropical attire: off-white jacket and knee-length shorts, topped off with a pith helmet. He was always accompanied by his similarly attired but diminutive wife, Esmeralda. While he went packless, she carried an enormous rucksack, from which, for some obscure reason, dangled a variety of kitchen utensils. The ramblers regarded them with, if not affection, then something approaching bemused tolerance.

Dan continued, "I've been leading for Goblick for nearly five years now. The numbers get ever larger, easily fill a train, sometimes seven or eight hundred. We even had a thousand on the Isle of Wight trip last year." He paused to chastise the tree again. "But there's never more than five or six parties. He says he can't find more leaders, but I don't believe he tries. He's been doing this job too long and got too set in his ways. Anyway, the sight of him, and his rude manner, are enough to put people off leading. I've had enough."

Rosalyn said, "Please don't stop leading, Dan. You're such a good leader and we'd be so sorry if you stopped."

"That's very kind of you, Ros, but I really can't go on like this. And another thing. He gets a commission from British Railways, so the more people who come, the more he earns. He doesn't care."

"I never knew that," said Winnie. "Surely that's not right. He ought to give at least some of it to charity."

"Him give to charity? Not a chance!" exclaimed Dan. "There's about a hundred in most parties. It's ridiculous! I only get fewer because I do longer distances, but even seventy or eighty is un-manageable. Then there's the lunch stop. Always too many people for one pub, so we have to try and find a place that's got more than one, which isn't always practical and limits the options. I even had to split my party between two villages once."

He paused for breath, bashing some more bracken. "And the party gets so strung out, it can take ten minutes for the rear to catch up. Now see what's happened. Alf has in effect stolen my party." He paused again, then: "And he wouldn't even realise, since he never bothers to count them. He's a rotten leader."

"So why do they go with him?" asked Percy

"Oh, Percy, don't be so naive!" scolded Rosalyn. "You've already pointed out that Ollie's been diverted by his rearguard, the gorgeous, lisping Tsubrina, Alf's niece. Most of his party are men, buzzing like bees around the pot of honey that is Tsubrina's ample bosom."

16

"Oh, her," said Percy. "Doesn't do a lot for me, I must say."

"I expect you're the only man on these rambles who thinks like that," observed Rosalyn. "Isn't he, Dan?"

Dan looked down at the ground and drew circles in the sand with his stick. "Well, I er….."

Rosalyn continued, ruefully "She probably undid another button on her shirt and Ollie was transfixed." She had noticed some attractive men among Alf's party, and resented Tsubrina's 'pulling-power'.

"Do you think her lisp is real?" asked Winnie. "I've always suspected it's put on."

"I wouldn't be surprised," agreed Rosalyn, with some bitterness. "Some men find it attractive." Winking at Winnie, she added, "I mutht twy it."

Dan, still doodling in the sand, stopped, grunted, gave the sand a mighty thwack and said menacingly, "Tsubrina's ample bosom indeed! That's the final straw. That does it!"

He drew a deep breath and continued theatrically, "Listen! For some time now, I've been thinking of forming a breakaway group. If I did, would you three come with me?"

"We're a breakaway group now," observed Percy, "and we're already with you."

Dan threw an exasperated glance skywards and said, "I mean, if I set up a rival excursion programme next year. Then we could have smaller parties."

"How would you let people know about it?" asked Winnie.

"Well, it wouldn't cost much to run off a few leaflets and pass them round on the trains this winter."

"That wouldn't please the Great White Hunter," said Winnie.

"I don't care what he'd think. Anyway, what could he do about it?"

"He could stop you leading again," said Rosalyn.

"But that's exactly what I want," said Dan, impatiently. "I don't enjoy leading like this. I only carry on because I don't want my regulars to feel let down. I'll spread the word amongst them at least – if I ever see them again after today's fiasco."

Dan paused and thought for a moment, then continued. "Henry and Peggy are leading Party Number Two today, but I'm sure they'd come, we're old pals. And they could spread the word amongst their group. We'd only need fifty or so to make it work, and a couple of leaders, then we'd have two, comfortable, manageable parties of around twenty-five."

"I'd come with you," said Rosalyn, adding thoughtfully, "And I might be able to persuade someone I know to come along. He once told me he doesn't like walking in large groups, so he might be tempted by smaller ones."

"I'll come too," said Winnie, who always did what Rosalyn did.

"Thank you, ladies. Percy?"

Percy stared at the ground and said nothing.

"Come on Percy," urged Rosalyn. "Are you with us?"

"I suppose so," replied Percy, morosely.

"You don't sound very keen," said Dan.

"Well, I only really come because I can't read maps," droned Percy. "If I could, I'd far rather be off on my own somewhere, taking photographs, birds and butterflies, wild flowers… that sort of thing."

"Thanks very much!" said Dan, offended.

"Take no notice, Dan," said Rosalyn, laughing. "I'm sure he appreciates our company really."

"Oh, it's not that I don't *like* you," said Percy, unabashed. "Nothing personal, just that I'd prefer to walk alone, if I could."

While they were talking, a distant metallic jangle grew louder. Then, around the corner, appeared

Dunsinane Goblick, the Great White Hunter in person. He and his wife always took a short walk in the area, separately from the main parties.

"Oh no!" muttered Dan.

Some moments later, the metallic jangle resolved into Esmeralda, with her enormous utensil-festooned rucksack. They included a small kettle, an aluminium teapot, a tea strainer, a bottle-opener, a corkscrew, a pair of sugar tongs, a set of folding cutlery, a pair of scissors, a whisk and a fish slice.

"Hello, Rose," said Goblick. "Lorst yer party?"

"As a matter of fact, yes I have," said Dan, triumphantly. "Alf Trayton stole it."

"What d'yer mean, stole it?"

Rosalyn intercepted. "He lay in wait at a junction, then when we came along, he pulled out a gun and ordered us to follow him. We four managed to escape."

"Don't be ridiculous!" growled Goblick.

Dan laughed. "It's not quite like that, but he's certainly got some explaining to do. You'd better ask him on the train home."

RRR

ROSE'S RAILWAY RAMBLES

Summer programme 1962

Welcome to the first season of Rose's Railway Rambles. We shall be offering a fortnightly programme on Sundays from May to September, and hope you will be able to join us. Here are the scheduled dates and times (fare for the return journey in brackets):

May 6th to Spindleford Halt and Stonegate (10s 3d).
Depart Charing Cross 9.50 a.m.
Return from Stonegate 5.55 p.m.

May 20th to Saxmundham and Aldeburgh (14s 6d)
Depart Liverpool Street 9.12 a.m.
Return from Aldeburgh 6.25 p.m.
Change Saxmundham homeward.

June 3rd to Gomshall and Guildford (9s 0d).
Depart Waterloo 9.45 a.m.
Return from Guildford 6.15 p.m.
Change Guildford outward.

June 17th to Ashurst and Eridge (10s 6d).
Depart Charing Cross 9.52 a.m.
Return from 6.33 p.m.

July 1st to Robertsbridge and Battle (13s 0d).
Depart London Bridge 9.32 a.m.
Return from Battle 6.50 p.m.
Includes free cream tea at Lindale Castle!

PTO

Continued from previous page

July 15th to Polegate and Eastbourne (12s 6d)
Depart Victoria 9.35 a.m.
Return from Eastbourne 6.45 p.m.

July 29th to High Rocks and Hartfield (10s 6d).
Depart Charing Cross 9.42 a.m.
Return from Hartfield 6.52 p.m.
Change Tunbridge Wells Central both ways.

August 12th to Pangbourne and Goring & Streatley
(11s 0d)
Depart Paddington 9.17 a.m.
Return from Goring & Streatley 6.22 p.m.

August 26th to Brockenhurst and Holmsley (15s 0d)
(bank holiday weekend)
Depart Waterloo 9.15 a.m.
Return from Holmsley 6.21 p.m.

Change Brockenhurst homeward.
September 9th to Canterbury East and Shepherds Well
(14s 0d).
Depart Victoria 9.37 a.m.
Return from Shepherds Well 6.25 p.m.

September 23rd to Berwick and Seaford (12s 6d).
Depart Victoria 9.47 a.m.
Return from Seaford 6.53 p.m.
Change Lewes both ways.

More information about the rambles will be available on
the outward train.

All details subject to change without notice.

Enquiries: Dan Rose ENF 9109

CHAPTER 2

ROSE'S ARE GO

Sunday 6th May 1962, 9.35 a.m.
Spindleford Halt and Stonegate

I

Dan Rose was standing at the entrance to Platform Two in Charing Cross Station, holding a white board. At the top, in bold black capital letters was printed "RRR". Below that, slightly smaller, "Rose's Railway Rambles". Then, handwritten, "Spindleford dep 9.50 a.m.", and at the bottom, "Front two coaches".

On the sleeve of his right arm was a red armband, bearing the letters 'RRR'. The publicity leaflets he had prepared also had 'RRR' at the top, so he hoped this would enable the ramblers to identify him.

Dan had spent much of the winter arranging his programme, and this was its first outing. A casual glance through the destinations revealed a marked preference for trips to Kent and Sussex: this was partly due to opportunities that had arisen, but having lived his first twenty-odd years in Tunbridge Wells, he knew the area well.

No special trains for RRR – he wanted to stay small, so they would use service trains with reserved carriages. Hastings was the eventual destination of today's train, but it would make an extra stop for the ramblers on the outward journey at Spindleford Halt, a little-used wooden platform between Wadhurst and Stonegate. They would return from Stonegate.

This was a bit of a coup for Dan, as the only trains that normally stopped at the halt were for the benefit of Henrietta, Dowager Marchioness of Goudhurst – Spindleford was the family name.

When the line was under construction in 1850, the second marquess had insisted that the platform be provided as a condition of crossing his land. Henrietta, the 87-year-old widow of the fifth marquess, was unable to travel much now, but had resisted all attempts by British Railways to close the platform.

The stationmaster at Charing Cross, a tall, rotund and kindly-looking gentleman in a very smart uniform and peaked cap, approached Dan.

"Everything alright, Mr Rose?" he enquired.

"Yes thanks. But I'm a little bit apprehensive, this being our first trip. It's only twenty minutes to departure and I've seen nobody yet."

"God bless you, sir, not to worry. There's a lot of people at the ticket office, and most of them look like they're dressed for a nice walk in the country."

"Oh, good. I don't want to be swamped, but we need a reasonable turnout to keep your employers happy."

The stationmaster was confident. "There's a good crowd. We've reserved the front two coaches for you, which gives you eighty seats. Will that be enough?"

"Oh yes, plenty. I'll be happy if we get fifty."

"And the train will make a special stop at Spindleford Halt, just as you requested, due 10.55. The platform's very short, so you must make sure all the passengers who want to alight there are in those front two coaches."

"Yes, I know, but thank you."

"And we have the written permission of her ladyship."

"Indeed. And more than that, she's kindly agreed to put in an appearance. But please don't tell anyone, I want it to be a surprise."

"My lips are sealed, sir. By the way, I see your board says 9.50, but the train actually goes at 9.55."

"Ah, that's just a little ruse to make sure everyone gets on well before departure. The leaflets I printed also say 9.50."

"I see. Well, that might cause a bit of confusion, but we'll see how it goes. Anything else I can help you with?"

"Can I leave this board here? I don't want to carry it around all day."

"Of course. Just leave it by the gate and I'll get a porter to put it in my office."

"That's very kind of you. The next trip's a fortnight today from Liverpool Street, but I'll pick it up well before then. Ah, here comes my son."

A tall, lanky young man appeared. Oliver Rose wore round, metal-rimmed National Health glasses, around which his unkempt light brown hair flopped, as if to form a protective barrier. Despite his youth, Oliver was a traditionalist and wore a tweed jacket and Paisley tie. Such wear had been quite fashionable for, indeed expected of, gentleman ramblers in the days before and immediately after the war, but by now most preferred a more comfortable pullover, or an anorak, and had dispensed with the tie.

Oliver came up to his father, held out a large envelope and said, "Hello Dad. Here are the itineraries. Mum ran them off this morning."

Dan's wife, Alice, was unable to walk far now, but happy to look after Dan and Ollie and get them out of the house occasionally. She had also helped with the organisation of Rose's Railway Rambles.

"Don't give them to me, boy! You'll be handing them out. Oh, just a minute, I'd better have a few." The itineraries consisted of a sheet with details of each party's leader, rearguard, route, lunch stop, and return train times.

A man and a woman came up, holding hands, though they were well into their sixties, with greying hair. Henry and Peggy Barden had run a little grocery shop in the East End, worked very hard and done very well from it, but now their son and daughter-in-law were in charge. So they could take expensive holidays and treat themselves to the latest walking gear, which today, for both of them, consisted of green anoraks, dark blue knee breeches, long black socks and very smart and shiny new boots.

Dan said "Morning Peggy, morning Henry. At least we've got a leader and rearguard, even if there's nobody to lead."

"Mornin' Dan, 'allo Ollie," replied Henry, who, having been born within the sound of the bells of St Mary-le-Bow, could claim to be a true Cockney.

"Good morning," said Peggy, in a precise Scottish accent that betrayed her Aberdonian origin, and added, "Don't worry, there's a crowd over by the ticket office."

Dan looked at his watch. "Hmm, well I wish they'd come over. I hate last minute scrambles."

"Most of them have already bought tickets," said Peggy. "They're just standing around chatting."

Suddenly, a piercing scream came from the station entrance. Then the stout lady who had emitted it entered the concourse, dragging Percy Fordingbridge by the ear and thumping his posterior with her umbrella.

"Ow," he shouted. "Let go of me!"

Seeing the stationmaster, the lady yelled, "Oi, you there, arrest this ruffian! He just assaulted me."

"I most certainly did not," protested Percy. "Your handbag caught a strap on my rucksack. I was simply trying to untangle them."

"More like your rucksack caught my handbag. Get on with it then!"

Percy continued fumbling, but the stout lady shouted, "You don't need to put your hands *there*! You're taking advantage of the situation." She hit him twice on the shoulder with her umbrella. "Help! Police! I'm being attacked. Get away from me, you fiend!"

Percy tried in vain to protect himself. "Ow! Ow! Madam, please! Stop struggling! I can't help while you keep wriggling so much."

"You're not helping in the least. You're just making it worse."

The stationmaster came to the rescue. "Please calm yourself, Madam. Here, let me do it." He quickly untangled the bags. "There you are. No harm done, I hope."

The stout lady was still quivering with rage. "Thank you very much. And no thanks to this idiot."

Percy bridled with indignation and boomed, "Well, that's a bit rich! If you hadn't kept hitting me I could have sorted it out in a jiffy, so it was your fault."

The stationmaster intervened. "Now then, madam, sir, let's leave it there, shall we? It's not worth getting into a tizz over."

The stout lady was still not done. "Hmmph. He should be locked up," she snorted, and flounced off.

Percy called after her, "I could have you arrested for assault." Her only response was to turn and wave her umbrella in a threatening manner.

The stationmaster looked at Percy. "Sorry about that, sir. Are you alright?"

"What? Oh, yes, suppose so," said Percy, rubbing his shoulder.

A crowd of ramblers had gathered round. "Poor old Percy," said one, amid laughter. "Always getting into trouble."

"You look like you're ready for walking, sir", said the station-master to Percy. Are you joining the ramblers' train?"

"Suppose so," said Percy morosely.

"Well, it's due to leave in fifteen minutes and there's the queue for tickets. You'd better join it, sir."

II

A few minutes later, ticket in hand, Percy joined the others at the entrance to Platform Two.

Peggy greeted him with a smile. "Hello Percy. Who was that lady we saw you with just now."

"That was no lady....." began Percy.

Henry cut in. "Don't tell me she was your wife." This reference to the corny old music-hall joke was lost on Percy.

"Of course not, I've never seen her before."

Dan laughed. "It's a joke, Percy."

Percy looked bemused. "I don't get it."

"Never mind," said Dan. "How did that job interview go?"

"No good. No surprise really."

"Oh, come now," said Peggy. "Surely a man of your education would've had no difficulty."

"Oh, there's no doubt I'm clever. Master of Arts at Cambridge, photographic memory, know the meaning and origin of every word in the Oxford English Dictionary."

"So what's the problem?" asked Henry.

"Clumsy, you see. Keep breaking things, messing things up. Probably some new species of human being. *Homo futilis*, that's me. Brilliant but totally useless. Sad waste of talent, of course, but what can I do about it."

"What a shame!" said Peggy. "What about working from home, couldn't you try that? There's lots of ads in the paper for people to work from home."

"Tried it. Soul-destroying. You end up packing things like wigs or incontinence pads. Even got sacked from the easiest job in the world."

"What was that?" asked Henry.

"Professional laugher."

"What on earth's that?" asked Dan.

"Paid to sit all day on the Circle Line, laughing at a book so that people would buy it. But the train was

31

so warm I kept falling asleep, then people assumed it was boring. But I'm going for an interview on Tuesday, which I'm quite optimistic about."

"Good for you," said Henry. "What for?"

"A clown with Perryman's Circus."

"You're joking!" declared Dan, amid much laughter from the others.

"Not at all. I come from a family of entertainers. All gone now, but Uncle Harry ran a troupe of acrobats. He and Auntie Flo performed on a trapeze and my mother was a tumbler."

"What was your father? A wine glass?" Henry's second joke, too, was lost on Percy.

"Good Lord no. He did tricks on a unicycle. Then he developed one that consisted of firing flaming arrows into the audience while riding the bike. Claimed they were guaranteed to go out in a second, but one night an arrow set fire to a woman's hat and it was banned."

"I'm not surprised!" exclaimed Peggy. "That's a ridiculous idea."

Percy continued, "I've got a good singing voice, actually. Baritone. Maybe I could join the young lads who sometimes stay in the flat above mine. They're musicians, just starting out. They're from Liverpool, so I can't understand much of what they say, but they're nice, polite boys. Don't know if you've heard of them. Call themselves The Beatles."

As the others shook their heads, a young man carrying a brief case approached. He had luxuriant, curly black hair and an upturned moustache and wore a blue pullover with a yellow diamond pattern, a white golfer's cap and smartly pressed blue jeans. He flashed a brilliant smile all round.

"Good mornings," he said. "Is for walking train?"

"Yes," said Dan, cautiously. "Is for walking train."

"Bueno. I..." The man placed his hand on his chest, bowed, and after a dramatic pause continued, "... am Joaquín Carlos Roca Diaz, from Caracas."

"Sorry?" said Dan.

Oliver attempted an explanation. "He said he's whacking Carlo's rocker, dears, and he's crackers."

Dan looked at Joaquín. "Why are you doing that?"

"Please?"

Dan did what many British people do when talking to a foreigner and said, loud and clear, "Why... are... you... whacking... Carlo's... rocker?"

Not to be outdone, the man shouted back, "Is... my... name. Joaquín... Carlos... Roca... Diaz."

Henry was incredulous. "Your... name... is... Whacking... Carlo's... Rocker? And you shouldn't call us Dears."

The young man looked totally bewildered, but Percy said with an exasperated air, "Oh, this is ridiculous. It's his name: Joaquín Carlos Roca Diaz. And he comes from Caracas, the capital of Venezuela." Then to Joaquín: "Bienvenido, Señor."

"Ah, gracias, Señor."

Dan said, "Percy, you dark horse. Didn't know you speak Spanish."

"Speak loads of languages. Hobby of mine. Twelve European ones plus Arabic, Japanese, Mandarin and Esperanto."

Peggy said, "Surely you could get a job as an interpreter, then."

"Trouble is, although I can understand them, they can't understand me. My accent, I suppose."

Henry said, "Look at his shoes!"

Percy looked down at his own walking boots and said, "What's wrong with them?"

"Not yours – Whacking's." Henry pointed at Joaquín's very smart brown and white brogues.

Joaquín was horrified. "Is my best shoes."

Dan said, "But you can't walk in those – they'll get muddy and scratched."

Joaquín was crestfallen. "So... I cannot come wiz you?"

Peggy took pity. "Don't be silly Dan, of course he can come. Whacking, you... are... very... welcome... to... come... but... be... careful ... where... you... put... your... lovely... shoes.

"Si, I will. If must, I will wipe behind."

Percy said, "I think he means 'afterwards'"

A small woman, who, though dressed in western fashion was clearly of an oriental provenance, came up to the stationmaster, made a perfunctory bow and said, "Please, where I get cow pong?"

The stationmaster, startled, said "I beg your pardon?"

Dan laughed. "You come with us, my dear, and you can have all the cow pong you want."

The woman turned to Dan, bowed and said, "Ah, so, you sell cow pong?"

Dan was nonplussed. "I don't *sell* it, no. What do you want cow pong for anyway?"

"I think, to get on train, I must have cow pong in hand. Or can I buy on train?"

As the others sniggered, the poor oriental woman, realising she had said something silly, blushed and lowered her head.

Dan threw his hands in the air and said, "This is becoming a farce. Percy wants to be a clown, Whacking wants to walk in his best shoes, now this young lady wants cow pong. What on earth is she talking about?"

Percy cut in impatiently. "Oh, it's obvious! She's trying to say 'coupon'. She wants a ticket!"

The oriental woman raised her head and gasped, then placed her hands together and bowed. "I am so sorry. Yes, tee-ket is right word. No, cow pong is wrong word, yes?"

"Very wrong word," said Dan, smiling. "You get tee-ket over there, where says tee-ket off-eece."

She bowed again. "Thank you, thank you. Tee-ket." And bowed again.

"You come with me, my dear," said the stationmaster. "There's not much time, I'll help you."

"Thank you, that is so kind." In her embarrassment, the woman could not stop bowing and repeating "Tee-ket."

Dan, Oliver, Peggy, Henry and Percy all bowed and replied, "Tee-ket."

Dan asked, "Where are all these foreigners coming from?"

Oliver said, "Probably the poster I put up on the notice board at my French evening class. There are foreigners learning English there too."

"I see," said Dan. "Well, I suppose it'll sell some more tickets.

"Stone the crows!" exclaimed Henry. "Look who's here! It's Tsubrina."

He nodded towards a strikingly pretty young woman with long blonde hair and an hour-glass figure that was accentuated by a rather tight and well-filled cheesecloth shirt and a pair of thigh-length khaki shorts.

"Oh good!" said Dan. "Here's our second leader."

"But that's Tsubrina Trayton," said Henry. "Surely she's not going to lead. Who's the feller?"

"That's her father, Luke," answered Dan. "He's leading, Tsubrina's his rearguard."

"But what about Uncle Alf?" asked Peggy.

"He had a heart attack last November and can't walk far now. He told me his brother wanted to be a leader. As it happens, I've known Luke for years. He was my batman in the army. Bit of a cheeky chappie but a good man. As none of Goblick's other leaders wanted to come over, I had to accept the offer."

"Couldn't you have led?" asked Henry.

"Prefer not. I've already got enough to do, organising the trains and making sure everything goes according to plan. But if a leader couldn't make it, then of course I'd step in and take over."

Peggy was concerned. "So aren't you going to walk?"

"Oh yes. I'll probably come with you and Henry, if you don't mind."

"Course not," said Henry. "Though we'll have to watch our step, with you hovering in the background."

"Don't worry," said Dan, laughing. "I won't interfere, and it'll be nice to walk without any responsibility, for a change."

Luke and Tsubrina joined them. Luke said, "Morning all. Everything under control, boss? I'm sure it is, knowing you."

"So far," said Dan, "but..." He stopped as a small group of walkers came up to the barrier, laughing loudly and pushing each other. "Oh, Lord!" groaned Dan. "It's the Happy Wanderers. We could've done without them. We'll get a bad name if they keep coming."

The Happy Wanderers were all almost identically dressed: baggy shorts, anoraks, red socks, heavy walking boots, and a bobble hat on every head.

A cheery, ruddy-cheeked woman called over. "Hello Dan. Bet you're glad to see *us*." It was Emily Bunticle, known as 'Bunty'.

Dan forced a smile and sighed. "Hello Bunty, er, glad you could make it. Now please hurry along and get in the first or second carriage from the front. "I hope... I mean, expect you'll be doing your own walk?"

"Oh, yes. We'll be having too much fun to tag along with you lot. Won't we, boys and girls?"

Someone shouted, "Three cheers for Bunty! Hip hip!" "Hooray!" "Hip hip!" "Hooray!" "Hip hip!" "Hooray!" And off they went, laughing and nattering, to the train.

Then, from a distance, could be heard the sound of an army on the march. "Left, right, left, right, left, right..."

Dan put his head in his hands. "Oh dear God, please not... Muttley's Marchers!"

All heads turned to stare as a group of nine marched across the concourse, in single file, all wearing military fatigues, forage caps and heavy boots. They were mostly men, but a very short one at the back, who was having difficulty keeping up, could have been female. At their head was a man carrying an officer's baton – the eponymous, pompous Major Muttley.

"... left, right, left, right. Halt!" The major came up to Dan, tucked the baton under his armpit and saluted. "All present and correct, Colonel! Where do you want us?" He knew that Dan had been a lieutenant colonel in the army, so acknowledged his superiority.

"Second coach from the front would be... "

"Yes, sah!" The major returned to the head of his column. "By the left, quick, march! Left, right, left... " And they trooped on to the platform, watched in amazement by everyone else on the concourse.

Dan's head was bowed and his eyes were tight shut. "I really didn't want this. We've got all the weirdos from the other lot."

Tsubrina slapped Dan's wrist playfully and said (with just the hint of a lisp and a little difficulty with the letter 'r'), "You mustn't call them weirdos, Mister Rose. It's derogatory. They can't help what they are. Maybe you think I'm weird because of the way I talk."

"Oh, no, my dear Tsubrina, not at all. It's just that they can be... well, embarrassing at times."

"Even so, we must treat all human souls with respect."

Dan sighed and smiled. "I'll try, my love, I'll try."

As Luke and Tsubrina set off along the platform, Henry said, "What a young woman like that is doing here beats me. You'd think she'd want to be with people more her own age."

Dan replied, "She told me she just loves walking, and she's very loyal to her father."

"She's training to be a teacher," added Ollie. "Her fellow students aren't interested in walking."

"And how do you know that?" asked Dan.

Ollie shuffled his feet and said, "She told me when I…" He was going to mention the time he accidentally strayed from Dan's walk, then thought better of it. "… a while ago," he finished, lamely.

"Huh!" snorted Dan.

"With that figure, she could be a model, or a film star even," said Henry.

Peggy punched his arm and said, "You would notice that!"

Henry smiled, looked at his watch and said "Gosh, Dan, it's almost departure time, we'd better get on the train."

"Ah," said Dan. "Actually, it's not leaving till five to now, but you're right – all aboard!"

As they walked along the platform, a group of young people ran past and climbed into the front coach.

"Who are they?" asked Peggy.

"Never seen them before," replied Dan. "But it's good to have some younger folk."

III

Rosalyn and Winnie had been standing by the ticket office. Rosalyn looked anxiously at her watch.

"I don't think he'll be coming now," she said.

"Who?" asked Winnie.

"My neighbour, Eddie. I was so hoping he'd come, to get him out of his shell. I knocked on the door this morning, but there was no reply."

"Why does he live in a shell?"

"Oh Winnie. You do make me laugh sometimes. You don't seem to have any idea of the real world."

Winnie flushed. She and Rosalyn had been best friends at primary school, but while Rosalyn had gone to a grammar school and university, and was now doing well in the City, Winnie had gone to a secondary modern. Being good with her hands, she now worked in her aunt's millinery shop. But they had remained close friends, and while Rosalyn tolerated Winnie's naivety with some amusement, Winnie stolidly put up with her friend's mildly barbed comments in the knowledge that they were not unkindly meant, and no offence was taken.

Besides, Winnie was very good at cooking, sewing, dressmaking – all the necessities of domesticity, in fact – while Rosalyn was hopeless at such things, and often had cause to be grateful for Winnie's help.

Rosalyn looked at her watch. "Nearly quarter to ten. Oh dear, he's not going to make it."

Winnie was still intrigued by Eddie's lifestyle. "So why does he live in a shell?"

"He doesn't actually live in a shell. It just means he's withdrawn, doesn't take an interest in things. His poor wife was killed in a car crash last year, and he's still grieving, naturally. I bet he's stuck himself in his office. He runs a small travel agency."

Winnie was shocked. "You mean he works on a Sunday?"

"Lots of people work Sundays these days. We're lucky, not having to. He immerses himself in work, trying to forget, I suppose, but it doesn't seem to help. He just mopes all the time. I suggested he should come with us today."

"And he said yes?"

"Sort of. They used to walk in Australia a lot, he and his wife. He's Australian actually, and they met while she was a secretary in the British High Commission."

"What's he doing here then?"

"She was British, and they decided to settle here. They did a lot of walking here too, and he had a sort of wistful look in his eyes when I suggested coming with us, so I thought, maybe he'd be tempted."

"Did they have children?"

"No, fortunately. Oh, no, I don't mean... that sounds awful, doesn't it? I mean, well... Oh, I don't know what I mean." Rosalyn was untypically flustered.

"You're in love with him, aren't you?" Winnie knew her friend well.

Rosalyn blushed. "No, of course not, whatever made you think that?"

"The look in your eyes."

"I'm just fond of him, that's all. I've known him for three years now. He's a nice, kind man, and I feel sorry for him."

Winnie kept quiet. She had seen her friend in the same situation several times before, then disappointed.

Rosalyn continued, "If he doesn't give himself a break, I'm terrified he's going to have a nervous breakdown, or a heart attack, or..."

"Catch German measles?"

"Don't be silly. How could anyone catch German measles from working too hard?

"Well, he works in a travel agency, so he might go to Germany and catch measles. Or Spain, and get bitten by a Spanish fly.

"Oh, Winnie, really! Do you have any idea what Spanish fly is?"

"I suppose it's a fly…. in Spain."

"Actually it's a beetle. And it's an aphrodisiac made from it."

"What's an afro….what you said?"

"It's…" Rosalyn looked despairingly at her friend and sighed. "It's a group of Masai warriors who perform a spinning routine on stage. An Afro dizzy act, you see? Oh, never mind."

The loudspeaker above them crackled into life, then made a noise that echoed around the concourse.

"The ttrraanngghhh nnooww ssttaannddiinngg aatt ppllaannggffoorrmmhh ttoonngghh iinnggss ffoorr Hhaassttiinnggss cccaaaallliiiinnnngggg aaattt Oorrppiinnggttoonn, Sseevveennooaakkss, Ttoonnbbrriiddgge, Ttuunnbbrriiddgge Wweellss Ceeentraaaall aanndd Hhaassttiinnggss. Aallssoo ssttooppiinngg ttooddaayy oonnllyy aatt Sssspinndddlleefforddd Hhaalltt"

Rosalyn looked at Winnie. "Did you understand any of that?"

"Of course," said Winnie. "She said 'The train now standing at Platform 2 is for Hastings, calling at Orpington, Sevenoaks, Tonbridge, Tunbridge Wells Central and Hastings. Also stopping today only at Spindleford Halt.' "

Rosalyn regarded her friend with astonishment. "Winifred Biddles, you never cease to amaze me!" She looked at her watch. "Oh crikey! The train goes in three minutes. Run!"

CHAPTER 3

WE'RE ON OUR WAY

Sunday 6th May 1962, 9.55 a.m.

I

As the train pulled out of Charing Cross, the ramblers were chatting about the day's prospects. Except Rosalyn, who was staring glumly out of a window.

A few minutes later, a deep voice with an Australian accent said, "Hello Ros, just made it."

A tall and very good-looking man was standing in the gangway. With his chiselled features, tanned face and dark, wavy hair that was starting to turn grey, he could have stepped straight out of an advertisement for men's clothing, if it wasn't for the old green pullover and battered grey trousers he was wearing.

Rosalyn looked up with a start, and it was like a ray of sunshine had struck her face. Her expression transformed instantly from gloom to delight.

"Eddie! You made it, well done!" she chirped. "Listen everyone! This is Eddie, my friend and neighbour." Then, to Eddie, "I thought you'd changed your mind."

"I overslept and was sure I'd miss the train," said Eddie. "I didn't even have time to get a ticket. It was nearly five to ten when I arrived, but I went to the platform anyway. The train was just pulling out, but the guard kindly let me scramble on and sold me a ticket."

Dan coughed. "I'm afraid that was a little ploy of mine, to get everyone on the train in time. The actual departure time was nine fifty-five."

"Well, you can't do that again," said Henry. "Otherwise we'll all assume we've got five minutes more than the time stated and end up missing the train. You'd better make that clear next time."

"Ah. Yes, I suppose so. Point taken, but the programme's been printed now, so we'll have to live with it for this season."

Rosalyn said, "Never mind that, Eddie's here and that's the main thing. Come and sit..." She stopped, looked past Eddie and groaned, "Oh no, it's Preston Twite."

The end door had burst open to admit a gormless-looking man with protruding teeth, straggly hair and several days' growth of beard. He came up to Eddie and confided, "It was the schooner Hesperus what sailed the wintry sea. A boy stood on its burning deck, his fleece as white as snow. He didn't know what time it was..."

48

Eddie, bemused, looked at Rosalyn for an explanation.

She said, "Alright, thank you Preston, we're having a private conversation here."

Preston made a noise that sounded like a flushing lavatory, but was supposed to be a laugh. He moved on, still chortling away.

"Oh dear," said Dan. "Sorry about that. I was hoping he'd stay with Goblick."

Rosalyn said to Eddie, "I'm afraid we get some rather barmy characters on these trips, and he's one of the barmiest. But these are my friends and they're all very nice and sensible. Winnie, Peggy, Dan, Henry, Oliver. Come on, sit down!"

"Thanks," said Eddie, and sat next to Rosalyn. "Pleased to meet you all."

"You're very welcome," said Dan. "Now then, Ollie, dish out those itineraries to everyone and count the number in these front two carriages." He turned to Henry and said, "Any problems on the survey? Happy with your route and pub?"

"All fine, thanks, we did the survey on Tuesday. Except that the pub's a bit, well, odd."

"In what way?"

"The landlord used to be a... well, he said hunter, but I've a suspicion he was a poacher. The pub's

49

full of stuffed animals in glass cases. Rabbits, chickens, a fox, etcetera. There's a stag's head on one wall, which is appropriate as it's the name of the pub."

"Actually, it was a lovely little roebuck," corrected Peggy. "I felt so sorry for it. But the landlord was very sweet."

"He was sweet on you, that's for sure."

"Oh, don't be silly, he was just being kind."

"Anyway," said Dan, "I must find Luke, to see how his survey went."

"He got in the third coach with Tsubrina," said Winnie.

Dan frowned. "Why the third coach? He knows we're in the front two."

"Why doesn't he come and sit with us?" asked Peggy. "There are spare seats."

"He had a newspaper," replied Winnie. "Maybe he just wants to read it."

"That's a bit unsociable," said Henry. "Are you sure you're doing the right thing with this Luke, Dan? If he's anything like brother Alf, you're asking for trouble."

"Well..." Dan seemed uncomfortable, and looked at the others. "I'll explain some other time."

Just as Dan started off to find Luke, the guard appeared.

"Sorry, Mr Rose. We've a bit of a problem. There are trespassers on the line at Petts Wood and we've been re-routed via Swanley."

"Oh dear," said Dan. "I suppose it'll delay us a bit."

"Only 10 minutes or so", said the guard.

Then Oliver burst breathlessly through the door. "There are trespassers... " he began.

Dan interrupted, "We know, the guard has just told us."

Oliver was disappointed – he liked to be first with news. "Oh. Well, anyway, it's great coz we'll be going along the Darenth Valley Line. It was opened in 1862 by the London, Chatham and Dover Railway..."

There were groans. "Here we go again," laughed Henry. Oliver was a train enthusiast and loved to show off his encyclopaedic knowledge of all things railway.

Winifred scoffed, "Thanks, Ollie, I've always wanted to know that, and I hope it gives you great pleasure."

"I love trains," said Oliver, unabashed.

"We know!" chorused the others, laughing.

Ollie ploughed on. "Next Sunday, I'm going on a special all-day excursion visiting stations with unusual names."

"Why?" asked Winnie.

"Yes, Wye's one," said Oliver.

"What do you mean? Where's it going?"

"Ware too."

"That's what I'm asking, where's it going to?"

"Yes. And Ore."

"Or what?"

"There isn't a Watt."

Winnie was getting annoyed now, and who could blame her?

Dan intervened. "Stop teasing her, Ollie! Winnie, the stations are called Wye, Ware and Ore."

"What soppy names to give to stations," snapped Winnie.

"They're not soppy," said Oliver. "They're the actual names of the places they're at."

Winnie was unimpressed. "And I think you're soppy to go on a journey just to see stations with soppy names. What will you do when you get there?"

"We'll take photos of the station name sign, and of the locomotive by the station name sign, and the stationmaster by the station name sign, and the driver and fireman by the station name sign, and the passengers by the station name sign, and the signal box with the station name sign on it, and..."

But the others were now discussing more interesting matters. "Right," said Oliver, meekly. "I'll hand out these itineraries, then."

II

In the third carriage, Luke was reading the News of the World, a Sunday newspaper that concentrated on the more lurid and sensational stories. Tsubrina sat opposite, flipping through the pages of Woman's Weekly.

The door opened, admitting Dan. "We're not good enough for you then," he chided.

Luke scowled. "Only wanted to read in peace."

"It would be nice to sit and socialise with the others. They don't know you. You could introduce yourself, maybe encourage some of them to come on your walk."

Luke smirked and jerked a thumb at his daughter. "They know her. They'll come on it!"

"Don't be so sure. Henry and Peggy are well known and popular. The regulars will go with someone they know, and they don't know you yet."

"I'll take my chance", said Luke.

"Well, you'll have to move forward when we get to Spindleford. You won't be able to get out from this carriage. Anyway, are you happy with your route and pub?"

"Why shouldn't I be?"

"As I explained to you, all sorts of problems can arise. Was your survey alright?

Luke shifted uncomfortably on his seat. "Well, actually, sorry boss, I didn't get round to it."

"Oh Luke! You promised you'd turn over a new leaf if I let you lead."

"I didn't promise, I said I'd try. I just didn't have time. Problems at work, had to sort out a strike. Anyway, I know the route like the back of my hand, and I've been to the pub loads of times. They know me there."

"But you can't just turn up unannounced with a large group. They might have some other group booked in."

"The place is huge, there'll be plenty of room."

"Well, I hope you're right. Please check it out in future. It's vital to know beforehand if there are any problems, to give us a chance of sorting them out."

Luke sighed. "Okay boss, I'll do my best."

From behind her Woman's Weekly, Tsubrina looked at Dan, smiled and shook her head.

CHAPTER 4

SPINDLEFORD HALT

Sunday 6th May 1962, 11.07 am

The train was actually twelve minutes late at Spindleford. When it stopped, the doors of the front two carriages were flung open and the ramblers spilled onto the little wooden platform. At the back was a low, wooden stockade fence, painted white, and in front of that was a line of trimmed bushes, alternately deep pink lilacs and yellow kerrias.

Luke threw open a door, leapt onto the platform and strode off. Dan was standing nearby and helped Tsubrina down.

"Thank you, Mister Rose," she said. "At least *you're* a gentleman!" She stuck her tongue out at her father's retreating back, then continued, "What a pretty little station! Thank you for bringing us here." Then, as they moved along the platform, she pointed and added, "Oh look! How wonderful, there's even a band to welcome us."

Indeed, in the forecourt, was assembled the Spindleford Brass Band in their smart green uniforms with red trimmings. Beside them stood a gleaming, silver-painted Bentley Mark VI limousine. An elderly chauffeur, standing beside it, opened a rear door, and helped the even older passenger get out. It was something of a struggle, for not only was Henrietta, Dowager Marchioness of Goudhurst, suffering from lumbago and arthritis of the hip, but a rich diet over nearly nine decades had played havoc with her proportions.

The chauffeur gave a hand to the Marchioness, but she lost her balance and tumbled out, pinning the chauffeur to the open door while he held her upright. If it had been a less well constructed vehicle, the door might have succumbed to the pressure, but this one held firm.

Her Ladyship said, "Thank you, Crombie." Then, holding the chauffeur's arm with one hand and a richly-decorated walking stick with the other, she walked slowly forward and threw a gracious arm towards the band. "Play!" she commanded.

The leader raised his baton and the band started to play. It was formed of folk from the Spindleford estate, mostly labourers and farmhands on French horns and drums, the blacksmith (flugelhorn) and the landlord (trumpet) and barmaid (trombone) from the Frog and Unicorn (features of the family coat of arms).

They had learned a medley of tunes connected with walking, but the members were all busy people and rehearsals were few and far between. The performance started well enough, which was just recognisably 'The Happy Wanderer', and this pleased the rambling Happy Wanderers no end, of course. They all knew the words and joined in lustily.

The second tune started off as 'Onward Christian Soldiers', but something went awry halfway, and the trumpet led the rest of the band into a cacophony. Eventually, the leader managed to restore some sort of order, by which time they were playing 'When the Saints Go Marching In'. As they ground to a halt, not quite in unison, there was a great cheer and applause from the ramblers.

The Marchioness applauded too and said to the leader, "Well done, Bindweed. That was much better than last time." Then she turned to the ramblers and said, "You're late." Before Dan had a chance to apologise, she continued, "Who is in charge?"

Dan shuffled forward. "I am, Your Ladyship," he said.

The Marchioness looked surprised. "Are you Rose?"

"Yes, Your Ladyship."

"I was expecting a female. Rose is a gel's name."

"It's my surname, Your Ladyship."

"Is she not here?"

58

The chauffeur whispered in her ear, and the Marchioness glowered at Dan.

"So you're Rose. Why didn't you say so, man?"

Dan looked awkwardly at his boots.

"And hold your head up!"

Dan snapped smartly to attention. "Yes, ma'am."

"Now, this is what you must all do. Turn left at the lane and march half a mile to the barn. There you will find everything you need. It is most kind of you to help us with the muck-spreading. Crombie, we shall now return to the house."

There was some consternation among the ramblers, but as Crombie led the Marchioness unsteadily back to the Rolls, he smiled at Dan, winked and shook his head.

The bandleader stepped forward, a portly, ruddy-faced, middle-aged man. In the delightful Wealden accent, gravelly-voiced, he said, "Sorry about that, folks. She seems to 'ave got 'erself muddled with tomorrow's lot. On 'er ladyship's be'alf, welcome to Spindleford, we're deloighted that the platform's bein' used, and wishes yer'all an 'appy day's raamblin'."

There were cheers and applause, and Dan started to speak, but the bandleader, interrupted.

"Boi the way, moi name's Sidney Boindweed. Oi'm not the usual baandleader, e's queer... That is, e's in bed with the flu, so oi'm staandin' in fer 'im. People calls me Staand-in Sid around 'ere, acoz oi'm always staandin' in fer people."

Sid beamed, the band members laughed and the ramblers clapped and cheered again.

Dan responded, "What a grand welcome. Thanks very much indeed, Mr Bindweed. We're truly honoured to have been welcomed by Her Ladyship and, er, serenaded, if that's the right word, by your excellent band." More applause and cheers.

Dan continued, "Now, we must get started. I suggest the private groups set off straightaway, then those who are walking with the official parties gather round their leaders."

Muttley's Marchers formed themselves into a column. The Major yelled, "Quick, march!" and they marched off. "Left, right, left, right... get out of our way!" Some of the ramblers were unceremoniously shoved aside by the Major.

Then Bunty Bunticle led the Happy Wanderers out, all laughing and cackling merrily, pushing each other, tapping each other on the head with their sticks. People made way for them, too – best give them a wide berth.

Then the group of youngsters ran past. "Who are you?" asked Dan of a petite young woman at the back, with black shirt and shorts, a tanned face and short dark brown hair.

"We are ze Mudlarks," she replied. in a French accent. "We go now to make ze quickest way to ze pub". And she sprinted off after the others.

"Haven't seen them before," said Dan to Tsubrina. "Good to have some young folk with us, isn't it, Tsubrina? Tsubrina?"

Tsubrina wasn't listening. She was looking wide-eyed at Eddie, who was walking past with Rosalyn. Tsubrina smiled at Eddie, who returned a half smile.

"Who's that man, Mr Rose?"

"Hadn't seen him before today."

"He's very handsome, isn't he?"

Rosalyn looked disdainfully at Tsubrina and whispered to Eddie "That's Tsubrina Trayton. Beware, she's broken many a man's heart."

"Not interested," laughed Eddie. "Much too young for me."

"That wouldn't matter to her."

"I'm sure she wouldn't go for a grey-haired old duffer like me."

"Just warning you. And just because you have a few grey hairs, it doesn't make you unattractive. Actually it makes you look rather distinguished."

Eddie gave Rosalyn a sideways glance. "Thanks," he said.

Dan climbed some steps by the platform and addressed the remaining ramblers, of whom there were about thirty.

"Right, gather round, everyone. I'd like to welcome you all on the first of Rose's Railway Rambles. I'm Dan Rose. Over there are your leaders: Henry Barden, for Party Number One...."

Someone shouted, "Good old Henry," and several cheered.

" ....and Luke Trayton, for Party Number Two."

Silence, though someone said, "Who?"

Dan continued, "Holding up the bats are their lovely rearguards Peggy Barden, for Party Number One...."

Accompanied by more cheers, Peggy held up a converted table-tennis bat, which had a big number '1' drawn on one side.

"..... and Tsubrina Trayton for Party Number Two."

A broadly smiling Tsubrina held up her number '2' bat to the accompaniment of wolf-whistles.

Dan said, "You see that we're substantially fewer in number than the other lot, especially as Major

Muttley and the Happy Wanderers are doing their own thing... thank goodness..." (laughter) "so the walking should be more comfortable, and the pubs less crowded."

Luke called out, "Get on with it. We're wasting time."

"Yes, alright, just a couple more things if you don't mind."

Luke muttered, "Oh no!" but Dan soldiered on.

"Please observe the usual rambling etiquette. Keep in single file along rights of way in cropped fields, keep to the right in single file on roads with no pavement, and don't wear muddy boots in the pub. In these respects, we're just like the other lot."

"Sod the other lot," muttered Luke.

Henry whispered to Dan, "Are you sure you're doing the right thing with this Luke, Dan?"

"Luke and I go back a long way," confided Dan. "We were in the army together during the war. He was my batman and saved my life once. I don't know what's eating him, but he said he was having trouble at work."

"I see," said Henry. "Well, it's up to you, but I think you're making trouble for yourself with him."

Eddie was standing on his own, at the back of the forecourt, while Rosalyn chatted with Winnie. Tsubrina came up to him.

"Hello, I'm Tsubrina." This was a slightly unfortunate name to give the girl, as it had turned out. Her speech defect made it more like Thoobweena, but she had learned to live with it.

"What's your name?" she continued.

"Eddie."

"Pleased to meet you, Eddie." She shook his hand and held on to it for rather longer than he felt comfortable with.

"You have an unusual name," he said. "Where does it come from?"

"Tsubrina's one of the mountains that Mummy and Daddy climbed on their honeymoon in Poland, near Zakopane, where Mummy was born." She hesitated and looked at the ground. "I think I was conceived there, actually. Anyway, I hope you're coming with us on Party Number Two."

"Afraid not. I'm with that lady over there, in the blue shirt. She's going on Number One, and it wouldn't be right if I didn't go with her."

Tsubrina could not hide her disappointment, and let go of Eddie's hand. "Oh. Is she your wife?"

"No, indeed not. We're just good friends and neighbours. I was married but my wife died in an accident last year."

Tsubrina took Eddie's hand again and said, "I'm so sorry. Daddy's a widower like you. Mummy died when I was eight."

"I'm sorry too. Rosalyn – the lady in the blue shirt – persuaded me to come today. She thinks it will do me good."

"I hope it will. I'm sure it will."

"Thanks." Eddie extracted his hand and looked around. "I think we're about to move off, so I'd better be... Oh, are you alright?"

Tsubrina had stretched her arms up, hands bent outward, with her face to the sky.

"I'm Daphne," she said.

"I thought you said Tsub... "

"And you're Apollo."

"Eh?"

"Apollo chased Daphne, but she didn't want to be caught and turned into a tree."

"I don't understand... "

"I'm turning into a tree. And trees give shelter to those in distress like you. Please be a branch on my tree." Tsubrina transfixed Eddie with an imploring expression.

Eddie stifled a laugh and said, "Er... that's very kind. Maybe some other time." He rushed away.

Luke came up. "Come on, Tsubrina! Stop messing about, we're ready to go." He glared at the retreating Eddie. "Who's he?"

"Yes, Daddy. See you later, Eddie," she called, and returned to Party Number Two with her father.

Eddie hadn't got far before Preston Twite approached and shouted, "Oi!" while raising an extended forefinger skyward, then took a sideways step towards Eddie.

Eddie stopped. "You talking to me?"

Now pointing at Eddie, Twite said again, "Oi!" and took another sidestep. "Oi! Are you the bloke what's in charge o' ramblin'?

"No," said Eddie.

"Oh. 'Oo are you then?"

"I'm somebody else."

Twite reacted as if a great light had been shone on the situation. "Aaoh! Well, where's the bloke what's in charge o' ramblin'?"

Eddie pointed at Dan. "I think you must mean the man over there, with the red armband."

Twite went over to Dan, repeating his oi-stride-forefinger routine.

"Oh, no!" groaned Dan. He tried to move away, but was too late.

"'Allo, mate," said Twite. "Didn't you die?"

"Obviously not," said Dan.

"I was told you'd died, so I just wanted to pay my respects."

Dan looked at the sky in despair and said, "Thank you, Preston, but we must get going."

Twite wittered on. "Is Barbara out today?"

"I don't know any Barbara."

"Yes you do! Wooden leg and a moustache. Plays for Accrington Stanley."

Dan regarded Twite with a mixture of incomprehension and scorn, then turned to the crowd. "Alright, everyone. Off you go, have an absolutely brilliant day."

He noted with relief that Twite was joining Party Number Two, then said to Henry, "I'm walking with you."

Oliver came up to Dan and said, "If you don't mind, Dad, I'm going with Luke."

Dan looked from Oliver to Tsubrina, then winked at Henry and said, "I wonder why."

Henry and Peggy counted their party. Peggy said, "I make it sixteen, including us," and Henry nodded. "So do I. Right, we're off."

Luke did not bother to count his party, but Dan noted that there were twelve, all men apart from Tsubrina. He fell in with Peggy at the back and said, "Not a bad turnout for our first trip. There are fifty-five of us, including the ones that went off earlier."

"Are you happy with that?" asked Peggy.

"Yes, very much, though it's a shame it includes the Happy Wanderers and Muttley and Preston Twite. Oh well, I think we've got enough to satisfy British Railways."

Henry set off to the right, while Luke went left. Tsubrina called out as they parted, " 'Bye Eddie! See you later." Eddie half raised a hand and half smiled.

Rosalyn frowned and said, "I see Tsubrina has got her claws into you already."

"She's mad", said Eddie. "Thinks she's a tree. And some other idiot thought I was the organiser. I see what you mean about barmy characters."

"That was Preston Twite. I suppose he should be pitied really. There's a screw loose somewhere, but he seems quite harmless."

A car drove up, a little too fast for the width of the road, and screeched to a halt in the station forecourt. The door opened and a handbag fell out, spilling its contents onto the ground. It was followed by a tall, thin woman with, presumably, dyed blue hair and spectacles. She yelled, "Wait for me!" and retrieved the items on the ground.

Dan was with Peggy at the back of Party Number Two. They stopped and waited.

"Terribly sorry," said the blue-haired woman, in an accent that suggested a public school education. "Late as usual. I'm Pandora Roade-Horlidge from the Kentishman magazine. Heard you were coming. Just wanted to ask a few questions and take some piccies, if you wouldn't mind."

"Alright", said Dan, looking at his watch. "But we're late already. Can you do it while you walk with us – for a while, anyway?"

"Fine, fine. Just carry on. I'll catch up."

Pandora put her bag on the ground and replaced the fallen contents, keeping hold of a notebook and camera. Then, just as she was closing the car door, a tractor drove past, towing a trailer piled high with silage. The tractor slowed to negotiate a bend, but not enough, it would seem, because a dollop of the malodorous cargo fell from the trailer onto Pandora. She sat on the ground in a daze, then burst into tears.

Dan and Peggy were so deep in conversation that they did not notice, and forgot about poor

69

Pandora. But one of Luke's party, a man in a tartan jacket, saw what happened. He was about to call after Dan, but thought better of it as his party had disappeared around a bend. He shrugged and ran to catch up.

CHAPTER 5

THE MORNING WALK

Sunday 6th May, around noon

I

Some two miles from Spindleford, Henry led Party Number One along a track between fields. Next came Rosalyn, chatting with the oriental woman, with Eddie close behind.

The soft sound of singing reached their ears and grew louder, resolving into the tune of 'Happy Wanderer'. Then the Happy Wanderers themselves came into view at a bend, walking in the opposite direction, with Bunty in the lead.

"Uh oh, here we go," said Henry.

Bunty could not have been more friendly, neither could the other Wanderers. It was just that, since most British people are somewhat reserved until a certain amount of alcohol has passed their lips, the Wanderers' excessive heartiness was really rather embarrassing.

"Hello, Henry," yelled Bunty, as she approached. "You're all going the wrong way. We're having such fun. Why don't you turn round and come with us? Ha-ha-ha." Henry forced a smile, waved and pressed on.

Bunty greeted every single member of Party Number One: "Good morning. Good morning. Good morning ..."

Eddie looked enquiringly at Rosalyn and frowned. She said, "The Happy Wanderers. They're bonkers, and I wish they wouldn't dress like that, all bobble hats and red socks, it gives ramblers a bad name." She paused. "You're not very impressed so far, are you?"

Eddie laughed. "I reserve judgement", he said.

They turned off the track at a stile. Henry crossed first, then Rosalyn. The oriental woman was next, but before putting her foot on the first step, turned to Eddie and bowed.

"Please, what is this called?"

"It's a stile," replied Eddie.

"Staa-eel. Please, will you take photo of me on it?"

"Of course".

She handed Eddie the camera that had been hanging round her neck and climbed onto the stile.

"Say cheese!" said Eddie.

"Please?" said the woman, uncomprehending.

"That'll do," said Eddie, the camera clicked, and he handed it back.

"Thank you. Please, what is your name?"

72

"Eddie. And yours?"

"Hitomi. In Japanese it mean 'middle of eye'."

"We call it a pupil."

"I think so, yes." Covering her mouth, Hitomi laughed, then said, "Is Japanese custom to give this name to girls with beautiful eyes."

"How charming," said Eddie. "If you take off your glasses I'll see if it's true."

Hitomi giggled and did as she was told.

Eddie said, "Yes, it's definitely true. You have very beautiful eyes."

Hitomi blushed. "You are very kind." She bowed, stepped down from the stile and walked on.

Rosalyn had been watching this little exchange, and as Eddie crossed the stile, said sarcastically, "How sweet," and added, "I noticed you didn't reserve judgement about that girl's eyes."

"I was just being polite," said Eddie, defensively.

"Well," said Rosalyn, sternly, "in my humble opinion, it isn't polite to gaze so closely into a stranger's eyes."

Eddie was rather taken aback, but Rosalyn smiled, slapped his wrist and walked on.

II

Meanwhile, what of Party Number Two? Luke, who had earlier asserted that he knew the route like the back of his hand, had managed to get lost. Worse, he had led his party along a path that narrowed to a dead end, and now they were strung in a line between a barbed wire fence and some hawthorn bushes. Their clothing had got caught and they could move neither one way nor the other.

Luke managed to extricate himself and, with the help of a fence post, climbed into the adjacent field. It was occupied by a herd of black-and-white Friesian cows, which observed the proceedings with a mixture of curiosity and mild alarm.

"Daddy," called Tsubrina, from the back. "I don't think this can be right."

Luke's response was to break wind with such force that the nearest cow bucked and ran off, starting a stampede.

"Wind!" yelled Preston Twite.

"Methane, actually," corrected Oliver.

The man in the tartan jacket, a Scotsman, said, "Whence bursteth forth obnoxious wind, cometh something more solid close behind.' After William McGonagle, *On Bodily Functions*."

A tall, gaunt, sad-looking man dressed all in black, said "I don't believe McGonagle wrote any such thing."

The Scotsman countered, "I never said he did. I said it was *after* McGonagle, so in his style."

"Who did write it then?" persisted the gaunt man.

"Nobody," said the Scotsman. "I just made it up."

Tsubrina had also managed to free herself, but in doing so ripped her cheesecloth shirt. Then she too climbed into the field and, while Luke stood watching, worked her way along the line of men, helping them get free. They were not exactly happy with their predicament, but in comp- ensation Tsubrina's torn shirt had exposed considerably more bosom than even she would normally dare reveal in public.

III

Back to Party Number One, now on a path that contoured through a steeply sloping woodland. Henry and Rosalyn were in front, engrossed in conversation. Next came Eddie, a few yards behind.

Suddenly, there was a whooping and a hollering. Some human forms emerged from the woodland above, crossed the path and disappeared into the bushes below. Two fell over, but apparently unhurt and laughing, quickly scrambled up and continued. But a small one, dressed in black, crashed into Eddie, knocking him to the ground, and came to rest on top of him.

"Oomph!" said Eddie.

"Oomph!" said the small person.

Removing itself from Eddie, the small person unfolded to reveal itself as the petite young French woman from the Mudlarks.

"I am so sorry," she said. "Are you alright?"

Eddie rose. "No bones broken."

"I think we were going too fast," said the Mudlark.

"You certainly were. But you seem to be enjoying yourselves."

"We run to arrive at ze pub more quick. It is very close now, I think. Oh, you 'ave much dirt on your clothes, I will clean zem."

Henry and Rosalyn had come back to see what all the noise was about.

Seeing Rosalyn, Eddie said, "No, please don't bother!" But the woman ignored him, brushing soil and leaves from his pullover.

"What is your name?" she asked.

"Oh," sighed Eddie, with a sideways glance at Rosalyn. "It's Eddie. Yours?"

"They call me Pochette. It means pocket in French. It is, 'ow you say, knickername, because I am so small. My family name is Saucy, which is a little village near Dijon, but also very appropriate for me." She raised her eyebrows and smiled.

Rosalyn said, "What happened?"

Pochette Saucy said, "It is my fault. I run too fast and knock eem over."

"I see," said Rosalyn. "You must have been travelling at some speed if a small but irresistible force like you can knock over a large but immovable object like Eddie."

Pochette ignored her. "Zat is all from your pullover, but there is still much dirt on your trousers."

"Right," intervened Rosalyn. "I think Eddie can manage by himself now. Hadn't you better be catching up with your friends?"

Pochette glared at Rosalyn and ran off down the slope. Eddie shrugged and spread his hands in a gesture that was meant to say, "Beats me!" Rosalyn frowned, then smiled, shook her head and walked on. Eddie followed in silence.

CHAPTER 6

AT THE STAG'S HEAD

Sunday 6th May 1962, lunchtime

I

The Stag's Head pub in the pretty little village of Badgerscombe was quiet for a Sunday, as most of its regulars had taken their drinks out to watch cricket on the nearby green. Only one table in the bar was occupied, by three elderly men playing dominoes.

One said to the man behind the bar, "Quoiet today, Reuben." The gentle Wealden accent was fast disappearing, but the regulars here still spoke it.

"It'll be a lot loivelier shortly," said Reuben. "There's a group o' raamblers on their way."

"Oh lor'! S'pose that'll mean clearing up the mud after 'em."

"Well, oi don't mind. 'S'not as if there's a caarpet. Oi've only got to sweep the floorboards. Any'ow, it's not rained fer a week, there'll be no mud."

Elsie, his wife, pointed through the window. "Here they are now," she said.

Henry led Party Number One through the pub's front garden. He stopped at the door, turned round and asked of his followers, "Well, what do you think?"

"It's perfect," said Rosalyn. "Pretty little village, beautiful garden, a pub with a thatched roof. Look, even a rose arbour there."

"Things *are* looking up," observed Eddie.

"Attention everyone," called Henry. "Unusually, we've found a pub that has food for a change. They do ploughman's lunches and toasted sandwiches. If you've brought your own sandwiches, please eat them outside, but at least buy a drink at the bar. If your boots are muddy, please either take them off and put them in the porch, or cover them over."

"Don't be silly, Henry," said Peggy. "We haven't seen a drop of mud all morning."

"Never mind that. I want the landlord to know we care. Anyway, they're dusty."

Rosalyn looked at her boots. "I don't suppose they're any worse than other customers. I'm keeping mine on."

"Oh all right," conceded Henry. "Keep your boots on if you like, but do make sure there's no mud on them. He glanced at his watch. We'll be leaving at a quarter past two, so that gives us just over an hour." He went inside and the others followed.

Henry said, "Good morning, landlord. Remember us? We were here on Tuesday and arranged to bring a party of walkers today. There are sixteen of us."

"Oh dear, oi'm afraid oi forgot all about it," said Reuben. He chuckled as Henry's face dropped.

"But..." began Henry.

"God bless you, sir, of course I 'ain't forgot. Just moi little jest. Lovely day you've got. Now what'll you 'ave?"

"A pint of best bitter please. What about you, Peggy?"

"Half of bitter shandy," she responded, "and we'll have two of your marvellous ploughman's lunches."

"Certainly, Madam. Elsie, get those, will you?" He turned to Joaquín. "What about you, sir?"

"I no like beer. You 'ave..." Joaquín gulped, took a deep breath and continued, "orranchay chwith?"

Reuben stared blankly. "Eh?"

Joaquín tried again. "Orranchay chwith."

Percy leaned forward. "I think he's trying to say 'orange juice'."

"Si, zat is it, sank you" said Joaquín, beaming at Percy and clasping him by the shoulders. Then he beamed at Reuben, said again "Orranchay chwith" and beamed at everyone else in the bar.

Reuben poured the juice and handed the glass to Joaquín. "Orranchay chwith for you sir", he said, smiling at Peggy. Then he turned to Winnie. "And for you, madam?"

"Just a lemonade with ice please. Do you serve peanuts?"

"I'll serve anybody, madam." It was his usual response to anyone who said "serve" instead of "sell". He looked around to make sure everyone understood his little joke.

But it was lost on Winnie. "Good. How about walnuts?"

Reuben was taken aback. "Lord save us! Oi've been in this trade for noigh on thirty year, and that's the first toime oi've ever been aasked for walnuts. No, we ain't got walnuts."

"Brazil nuts, then?" persisted Winnie. "I like nuts."

"No brazil nuts noither. And before you ask, no hazel nuts, cobnuts, almonds or chestnuts noither."

"Oh. Just the lemonade and peanuts then, please."

Reuben looked at Henry, as if to ask if all the ramblers were like this. Henry just smiled and shrugged.

Percy was next.

"And what are you 'avin', sir?"

Percy was sitting on a stool by the bar, balancing on its front legs. "See you've got Tankerton's Red Shield. I'll have one of those, but be careful how you pour it."

"With respect, sir, oi've been pourin' Red Shield for donkey's years. Think oi've got the 'ang of it be now." Reuben opened a bottle and started to carefully pour the amber contents into a glass.

"Crud?" enquired Percy.

"Pardon?"

"Crud still in bottle?" continued Percy, in his cryptic fashion.

Reuben held up the bottle so that Percy could see that there was still sediment at the bottom.

"Per'aps sir would loik to finish pourin' it 'isself?" he said, with more than a little touch of sarcasm. He was getting a little tired of Percy's lack of faith in his professional ability.

Percy was insensitive to the landlord's feelings. He took the bottle, then in leaning forward to pour, the stool shot back, Percy fell off, came to a rest with his chin on the counter, but in doing so poured the rest of the beer into the glass, crud and all.

"Bugger!" yelled Percy.

"Language, sir!" smirked Reuben. "You should 'ave let me finish. Oi'm afraid oi'll still 'ave ter charge you for that, sir. A shillin' and sixpence, please."

"What, for swearing?"

Reuben laughed. "God bless you, sir, no. If oi charged ev'ry time someone swore in 'ere, oi'd be a millionaire be now. That's for the beer, sir."

A muttering, reluctant Percy handed over the money.

Fortunately for the reputation of ramblers in general, the orders from the rest of the party were for more usual refreshment. Henry, Peggy, Dan and Percy sat at a table inside, while most of the others went to sit in the garden.

Some minutes later the phone rang and Reuben answered. "G'd arternoon, Stag's Head."

A very loud crackling noise came down the phone — enough to make Reuben hold the receiver away from his ear.

"Yes sir," he said. "Certainly, sir. Noine 'alves of bitter, sir, thirteen fifteen hours precisely, sir. They'll be ready sir."

The loud noise sounded again. "It'll be eleven shillin's and threppence, sir." Reuben replaced the receiver with a trembling hand.

Unusually for him, landlord Reuben was visibly shaken. "What does thirteen fifteen hours mean?" he asked of Dan.

"That's one fifteen p.m."

Reuben looked up at the pub clock. "Oh lor', that's just over 10 minutes. Better get pourin', Elsie!"

II

Rosalyn, Eddie and Winnie had found a table with a sunshade in the garden.

"This is lovely," said Rosalyn, with a contented smile. "Beautiful sunny day, excellent pub, good beer, food and wonderful company. What more could a girl want?"

"Love," said Winnie.

Rosalyn stared at her friend. "Winifred Biddles! That's the first time I've ever heard you express such a wish."

"I'm not talking about me," said Winnie.

Rosalyn coughed and changed the subject. "Look, there are concentric rings on my beer."

"Mine too," said Winnie.

"And mine," said Eddie. "Wonder what's causing that,"

"What's that noise?" asked Winnie.

"I can't hear anything," said Rosalyn.

"Sounds like an army on the march," said Winnie, whose hearing was very acute, as we have already learned.

She was right. Moments later came a rhythmic chant, "Left, right, left, right, left, right... " and into view hove the unmistakeable figure of Major Muttley, followed by his platoon. They marched along the garden path, the Major flung open the door and the Marchers stamped their way into the bar.

III

Dan had just said to the others, "This a is a nice, peaceful little place" when the door was thrown open and in marched Muttley, followed by his Marchers in single file. Conversation ceased and everybody in the bar stared in amazement. One could almost hear martial music accompanying the clomping boots.

Reuben was pouring the last of the nine half pints. Muttley reached the bar, grabbed a glass, and threw its contents down his throat. All the while he marched on the spot, as did the whole platoon behind him. Slamming the glass back down on the counter, he thrust a pound note into the hand of the landlord and roared, "Change to the back!" Then he marched on to leave by another door.

One by one, the platoon members followed suit and marched out. Except that the little one at the back, of indeterminate gender, and struggling to keep up, in throwing the beer back missed the target and got most of it over his or her own face.

Reuben was standing, mesmerised, with the pound note still in his hand. The little Marcher snatched the note and marched out. With a start, the landlord regained his senses. "Oi, come back, you 'aven't paid," he called, and ran out. But there was no stopping Muttley's Marchers, they had disappeared down the lane.

Dan said, "Oh dear, so sorry about that. I feel responsible for them, God knows why." He took a pound note from his wallet and handed it to the landlord. "Here, take it from this."

Reuben said, "Oh, no, sir, oi couldn't. It's moi own silly fault."

Dan said, "I insist. I'm sure we'd like to come back here someday, and I don't want us to get a bad reputation."

"That's very kind of you sir, but oi don't think....."

Peggy said, "Why don't you go fifty-fifty? That would be fair."

"Well, all roight," said Reuben.

"Okay," said Dan.

IV

An hour or so later, Dan, Henry and Peggy were returning glasses and plates to the counter.

"Time to go, I'm afraid," said Henry.

"Best ploughman's I've had for ages," said Peggy.

"Thanks very much," said Reuben. "Been a pleasure to 'ave you... well, most of you, anyways. "Oi 'ope you'll be back soon."

"I'm sure we will," said Dan.

"And where moight you be walkin' to this afternoon? If you don't moind me aaskin'," enquired Reuben.

"We finish at Stonegate, going via Coppice Farm and Mellow Mere," said Henry. "It's about five miles, the way we're going."

Reuben frowned, shook his head and clicked his tongue. "Coppice Farm? Not a good oidea, sir, if oi may make so bold. Nor Mellow Mere, noither."

Why not?" said Peggy. "We had no problems when we checked the route on Tuesday."

"Oh ar, you'd be all roight on a Toosday 'cos ol' Faarmer Maandrake goes to maarket. But 'e'll be at 'ome now."

"So what?" said Henry.

"'E'll see you this toime, that's what. And 'e don't loike visitors, do ol' Maandrake."

Henry was indignant. "But it's a public footpath through there. Several paths, actually, all converging on the mere. It's a beauty spot."

"That don't make no difference to ol' Maandrake. 'E only took over the place a couple o'month ago, when 'is ol' pa paassed away. Mellow Mere's 'is own proivate property, 'e says, an' e's not lettin' strangers in."

"He can't stop us," spluttered Dan. "If he wants to close the public footpaths he must go through the proper channels, and that takes time. We're going that way, and if he tries to stop us he'll be breaking the law."

"Well, don't say oi didn't warn yer," said Reuben. "If you take moi advoice you'll go another way."

"We can't," said Henry. "That's the shortest way and we haven't time for a diversion. We'd miss our train."

The door opened, and in came a ragged Luke: shirt and shorts torn and, horror of horrors, mud on his boots.

"Hello Dan," he said. "I was hoping... er, expecting you'd have gone by now."

"Stop right there!" commanded Henry.

Luke stopped right there. "What?"

"Take off those muddy boots, that's what," said Henry, quietly, but in a menacing tone.

As Luke reluctantly removed his boots, Dan said, "What are you doing here? I thought you were going to the Black Bull."

"Yes," said Luke. "But they, er, they let us down."

Reuben said, "God bless you, sir. The Black Bull's been closed this last month. They 'ad a fire, they did. Some say it'll be months before it reopens."

Luke glared at Reuben.

Dan said, "It's your own fault, Luke. If you'd done your survey as I asked, you'd have known that and made other arrangements."

Luke advanced to the counter, saying "All right, all right."

Henry whispered to Dan, but loudly enough to be heard by Luke, "Looks like you might need to find another leader."

"You take that back," said Luke. "It was just a bit of bad luck, that's all."

Peggy, ever the practical one, said, "Boys, boys! Calm down. There's no problem. We're going now, so Party Number Two can get their lunch and our friend the landlord will get twice as much business as he expected."

"Well, not exactly, m'dear," said Reuben. "You've cleared us out. There's only peanuts and crisps now."

"You greedy pigs!" exclaimed Luke.

Peggy was angry now. "Well, I like that! It jolly well serves you right."

Dan said, "Now then, you lot, cut it out. We've got to go."

Percy was sitting on a bar stool, observing the proceedings in a detached manner. "Funny thing to say, isn't it?" he said.

"What's funny about it?" asked Dan.

"I mean, 'Now then'. It's nonsense, isn't it? Now means now and then means then. It's like saying 'Here there' or 'Yes no'".

Luke was exasperated. "What's he blathering about? Talk sense, man!"

"That's exactly what I was doing," protested Percy. "I was commenting on Dan's grammar."

"Well, you've lost me," said Henry. "Anyway, it *is* time we went. Thanks very much, landlord. Hope to see you again, some time."

"Thank you, sir, we'll be deloighted."

Dan turned to Luke and said, "We'll talk about this on the train home."

V

The rest of Party Number Two were waiting in the garden for further instructions from Luke. The reason they had not deserted the sinking ship – Tsubrina – came up to Eddie, sitting with Rosalyn and Winnie.

Tsubrina's earlier encounter with the barbed wire and hawthorn bushes had not only left a great tear in her shirt but torn off a couple of buttons, and it was now undone to well below brassière level. She bent over and leaned on the table in front of Eddie.

"Hello Eddie. We had to make a diversion. Our pub burned down."

Eddie studied his empty glass, trying not to look at Tsubrina's cleavage. "How sad. You all look like you've had a rough time. What happened?"

"We got caught on some barbed wire."

Rosalyn said, disapprovingly, "For goodness' sake, Tsubrina, you're indecent. Haven't you got a safety pin or something?"

"No," said Tsubrina, pouting.

"I have," cried Winnie. She always carried a sewing kit, wherever she went. Burrowing into her ruck-sack, she extracted it.

Rosalyn continued, "And whose idea was it to come here?"

"Mine," said Tsubrina.

"What a surprise!" retorted Rosalyn.

Winnie triumphantly passed a safety pin to Tsubrina, who gave it a bemused look then put it in a pocket. She said to Eddie, "Why don't you come with us now, Eddie."

Eddie said, "I'm sorry, I can't. As I told you before, I'm with this lady."

"Hard luck!" said Rosalyn to Tsubrina.

"Why did you say that?"

"Oh, I don't know. I just got the feeling you were expecting a different answer."

"I don't know what you're talking about." Tsubrina sighed and said, regretfully, "Oh alright. I'll see you on the train home."

Henry came to the table. "Come along, you three, we're off."

Rosalyn glared at Tsubrina and thought, "You tart!", but said, "Enjoy your afternoon walk, Miss Trayton. Goodbye."

Tsubrina returned the glare and thought, "You don't stand a chance against me", but said, "Yes, I'm sure we will. Goodbye, Mrs... er... sorry, I don't know your name." Then she smiled at Eddie and said, "Goodbye, Eddie, see you later."

CHAPTER 7

MELLOW MERE

Sunday 6th May, around 4 pm

I

Joaquín, who had been walking near the back of the party, caught up with Winnie.

He said, "Please, what is your name?"

Winnie, who was always shy and awkward with men, said guardedly, "Winifred."

"Winifred. Is lovely name," said Joaquín. Then, placing a hand on his chest and bowing, "I am Joaquín Carlos Roca Diaz." Then added proudly, " I come from Caracas in Venezuela."

"Where's that?"

Joaquín was shocked. "You no heard of Venezuela? It is most beautiful country in South America. Beautiful cities, beautiful beaches, beautiful mountains, beautiful lakes, beautiful rivers…" He was going to add "beautiful women" but discreetly decided against it and continued, "You must come for holiday."

Winnie laughed. "Oh, I could never afford to go to South America. Why are you here?"

"I come for work experience. My father owns big shop in Caracas, I sink you say 'department store'. He send me to work for one year at Partridges in Oxford Street."

"Ooh, that's nice," said Winnie. "I sometimes go there to look at the clothes, jewellery and perfume, but I could never afford to buy anything."

"Next time you come, you ask for me. If I am free, I buy you coffee in ze staff canteen."

Rosalyn, walking just in front of them with Eddie, overheard this exchange, gasped and smiled. It was the first time she had ever known her friend to be chatted up by a man.

But Winnie was embarrassed and confused. She had never received such a proposition before. "Well, I don't think..." she began.

Rosalyn turned round and said, "Oh, go on Winnie. I'm sure Whacking is a perfect gentleman."

"Si," said Joaquín, with a broad smile. "I am famous in Caracas for being perfect gentleman."

"Well," said Winnie. "If I go there again I'll think about it."

They were now in the middle of a wood. Peggy, from the back, called out, "Henry, some of us need a comfort stop. This looks a good place."

Henry laughed. "You've had too much beer."

"Certainly not! There was only one ladies' loo at the pub and such a long queue, it would have taken ages for us all to go."

"All right, of course we can. Are we all here, love?"

"All present and correct."

"Right then." Henry cleared his throat, shouted, "Gentlemen, fifty paces forward!" and started to walk on. "One, two..."

Eddie said, "Hold on! What's all this about?"

"It's the custom, Eddie," replied Henry. "A diplomatic gesture by the men to give the ladies a chance to dive into the bushes to... er, relieve themselves. With no possibility of being disturbed by a gentleman of the opposite gender with the same purpose in mind."

"Well, actually," said Eddie, "I do rather want to relieve myself too."

"You can do that when we've done the fifty paces," said Henry. "So, gentlemen, fifty paces forward! One, two, three, four..." The men set off, and the women dived hurriedly into the bushes.

A minute later: "...forty-eight, forty-nine, fifty." On "fifty", all the men dived hurriedly into the bushes.

Nobody had thought to explain to Hitomi and Joaquín what was going on, but they soon grasped the idea. Having each been last of their gender group to start the proceedings, they found the nearest spots engaged, and had to keep moving on till they found a vacant spot. And, would you believe it, they were both using the same large tree, one on either side.

There is a well-known Mexican folk song that tells the sad tale of a cockroach that has lost a leg. As Hitomi dropped her trousers, Joaquín was so happy to relieve himself that he burst into song: "La Cucaracha, la cucaracha," he warbled. Hitomi screamed, pulled up her trousers and ran off.

Joaquín was mortified. "O calamidad! Calamidad! Perdoname, señorita!"

II

Half an hour later, Party Number One reached Coppice Farm. The actual farmhouse, a little way back from the road, was dilapidated, with a derelict garden in front.

Henry waited at the point where they had to leave the road, in order to follow a track – the one that Henry knew was a public footpath, leading to Mellow Mere.

When everyone had caught up, he addressed them. "Right, listen everyone! There's a rumour that the farmer here objects to walkers on his land, but this track's a right of way and he can't stop us.

96

And the map shows it's a public footpath too, so we're going to use it."

Rosalyn said, "Are you sure about this, Henry. Maybe we should stick to the road."

Henry said, "Rab-dab-dab!" — an expression he used when exasperated. "Don't be such a faint heart. We're ramblers. We may seem harmless, but we always get our way in the end.

"Look at the Mass Trespass on Kinder Scout in 1932. We're following in their footsteps. You don't get anywhere by being faint-hearted. And anyway, we must go this way, or we'll miss the train." This was a long speech for Henry, and there was some applause.

"Well said, Henry," said Dan. "He's quite right. I checked with the council and this is definitely a right of way. No cause for concern at all."

A dog started barking, though it seemed rather half-hearted, as if it was all too much of an effort on such a warm day. Then the front door of the farmhouse opened to reveal a short, stocky, ruddy-faced man in a tattered jacket, baggy old trousers and battered pork pie hat. It was Farmer Mandrake. He shouted, "What's all this noise? What you lot think yer doin', staandin' there?"

"Oh dear, I don't like the look of him," said Winnie.

Henry was emphatic but diplomatic. As Mandrake approached, he said, "Good afternoon, sir. We're just about to follow this... *public*... footpath."

But diplomacy was lost on Mandrake. He came right up to Henry and said, menacingly, "There ain't no public footpaath 'ere."

Henry took one step back, slightly less sure of himself. "Er... I think you'll find there is. It's... it's on the map. Look!"

"Oi carnt read maps. Oi tell you there's no footpaath."

Dan chipped in, "I assure you there is. The council confirmed it."

Then Percy yelped. "Ouch! My leg just hit something hard in the grass. Oh, look! A lump of concrete."

"Let me see that!" said Henry. He pushed the grass aside and heaved up a concrete sign bearing the text 'public footpath' and an arrow. "See!" he exclaimed, triumphantly. "Someone's pulled this out then tried to hide it." Then, to Mandrake, "Did you do that?"

Mandrake looked uncomfortable. "Oi told the council to move that, an' they took no notice, so oi did. There ain't no footpaath 'ere, an' that's the end of it. On yer way, use the road."

Then Mandrake caught sight of some broad tyre marks going down the track. " 'Ere, did you lot do that?"

Percy laughed. "Now how do you think we could've done that? Like this maybe?" He shuffled sideways to make something like a track.

"Less of yer lip, mister! Oi'm goin' to foind out 'oo made them tracks."

There was more sad barking from the house, and Mandrake scowled. "If moi darg weren't lame oi'd a-set 'im aan yer." He went back inside.

A car drew up alongside the party. The window was wound down and a mop of blue hair appeared.

"Hello there!" it said. "Caught up with you at last. Wait for me!" It was a somewhat dishevelled Pandora Roade-Horlidge, the intrepid correspondent from the Kentishman magazine.

Henry ignored her. "Right," he said. "Here's our chance. Quick, everyone, walk fast behind me and keep close together."

"Oh Henry," said a vexed Rosalyn. "Perhaps not, he looks dangerous."

"It's either this or we miss the train. Now come along!"

Peggy backed up her husband. "There's thirteen of us and one of him. What can he do? Let's go!"

Party Number One reluctantly fell in behind Henry as he set off down the track. But no sooner had Peggy, the backmarker, dutifully fallen in at her post at the back, than Mandrake emerged from the house, carrying a double-barrelled shotgun.

"Oi! Oi!" he screeched. "Come back' ere. Git orf moi laand. Oi'll git you, see if oi don't." Then he set off in pursuit, waving his shotgun in the air, but his age and build resulted in much slower progress than the fitter ramblers.

"Oh, Lord," screamed Winnie. "He's got a gun." And as of one mind, Party Number One broke into a run.

Pandora had got out of her car. "Cripes!" she exclaimed, on seeing the shotgun. "I've got a scoop."

She returned to the car, extracted a notebook and camera and set off down the track after Mandrake. Being younger and faster, and bearing the shotgun in mind, she kept well behind him, stopping occasionally to take pictures.

III

At the foot of the track from Coppice Farm, only a few hundred yards, was an idyllic spot by a large pond, almost a lake at some 200 yards across. This was Mellow Mere. It was just too lovely to be enjoyed by just one person, especially when that person, Farmer Mandrake, had such little regard for the more beautiful things in life. Nevertheless, it was legally Mandrake's property, and the igloo should not have been there.

Henry, at the head of Party Number One, was of course the first to see the construction, and stopped suddenly. He had no choice, because it had been erected beside the lake, almost blocking the track. Eddie, Rosalyn and Hitomi were very close behind, and they all crashed into Henry, to become a tangle of arms and legs on the ground. The others managed to stop in time to avoid becoming enmeshed.

Percy caught up. "It's an igloo," he observed, unnecessarily.

"I can see that," said Dan, but what the blazes is it doing here?"

"Never mind what it's doing here," gasped Henry. "We've got to get round it to reach the road, and once we're on that he can't touch us."

Then one of Joaquín's lovely shoes got caught in a patch of mud beside the mere.

"Ayúdame!" he yelled. "'Elp!"

Hitomi, being nearest, recognised the alarm in his voice, and ran back. She started pulling one of Joaquín's arms, but the shoe was firmly stuck. Winnie went to help, and pulled on the other arm.

Eventually, Joaquín came free, but the shoe was still stuck in the mud. Henry found a stick and poked around the reluctant shoe, eventually freeing it.

But Mandrake had caught up. "Gotcher," he shouted, pointing his shotgun at Joaquín, who put his hands up, and the rest of Party Number One followed suit.

Then Mandrake saw the igloo. "What the....." he spluttered, pointing his shotgun at it.

Up came Pandora. "Could you please turn to your left a little?" she asked. "Then I can get your gun in the frame."

Mandrake swung round and pointed the gun at Pandora. All due credit, she did not flinch, did not put up her hands, and got her picture.

"You stop that," yelled Mandrake. "Gimme that camera!"

"Shan't!" Pandora held her ground as Mandrake took a menacing step towards her and tried to pull the camera away, but its strap was round her neck and he only succeeded in pulling her towards him. There was a brief struggle, and several ramblers tried to intercede. Then the strap broke and poor Pandora fell backwards into the mere, but had the presence of mind to hold the camera clear of the water, before clambering out.

Mandrake turned and pointed his shotgun at the ramblers. "Roight, you lot, now clear off back up the track, the way you came."

As has been noted, Mellow Mere was a truly delightful spot, and several footpaths converged there. It was from another of these that Party Number Two emerged.

Tsubrina called out, "Hello Eddie! Why are you all holding up your hands?" Rosalyn scowled.

"What the....." spluttered Mandrake, pointing his shotgun at Tsubrina, who put her hands up, along with the rest of her party.

Then, from another direction, came the sound of singing. "We love to go a-wandering along the mountain track," they informed the world at large, whilst emerging from a third path.

"What the....." spluttered Mandrake, pointing his shotgun at Bunty. The Happy Wanderers all put their hands up.

Then, with Pochette Saucy at their head, the Mudlarks emerged from the same path as Party Number Two, laughing and shouting

"What the....." spluttered Mandrake, swinging his shotgun round. The Mudlarks put their hands up.

The sound of Muttley's Marchers usually filled the other ramblers with dread, but this time it was welcome, coming down the track from Coppice Farm. "Left, right, left, right....."

Mandrake, under the impression that the army was approaching, swung round to face them and fired a warning shot up to the sky. The pellet struck an unfortunate wood pigeon, which fell and hit Mandrake on the head.

"What the....." he spluttered.

Mandrake was now surrounded by fifty-three ramblers. All this time, unnoticed due to the commotion, a man in a kayak had been paddling across the mere. Suddenly he gave a triumphant shout and held a spear in the air, on the end of which was skewered a large, lifeless fish.

"What the....." spluttered Mandrake. But it was to be his last splutter. He managed a few more words, though they were very faint. "'E's got that poik, what's been eatin' orl moi carp. Oi bin troying to get that poik fer months, and 'e's got'n."

He gasped, clasped his chest, and with an "Aaaargh" staggered forward and crumpled in a heap on the ground.

Peggy said, "Stand back, everyone! It may be a heart attack. Don't crowd him." She felt his pulse, then extracted a mirror from her rucksack and held it to his mouth. "Oh dear Lord! I think... I'm afraid... I'm sure... he's quite dead."

There was a shocked silence, then Percy said, "Too much excitement for the poor old boy."

Henry snorted and said, "Poor old boy, my foot. Serves him right."

"Henry!" scolded Peggy. "How can you say that? Have a bit of respect for the dead."

Rosalyn said, "I agree with Henry. He was a danger to all and sundry, including himself. Don't you think so, Eddie? Eddie?"

But Eddie had turned his attention to the igloo. "What on earth is this doing here anyway," he said. He went to the entrance tunnel that stuck out several feet from the main part of the structure, and peered inside. As he did so, a young woman crawled out, almost bumping into him.

Although wearing a very pretty flowered dress and sandals, she was clearly of Mongolian stock, so Eddie was astounded when she said, in broad Cockney, "Wotcher cock!"

"I beg your pardon!" exclaimed Eddie. "Where did you learn to talk like that?"

"London School of Economics, tosh. I studied there for three years and stayed with a family in Whitechapel. You ain't no snob, are yer?"

"Er, no. I'm just surprised. Actually, it sounds rather attractive. But what are you doing here. What's this igloo doing here? Surely it's not ice."

105

"Nah! Course not." She tapped the roof. "Plastic, innit. My ol' Grandpa wanted to see England before 'e snuffed it, but wouldn't stay in 'otels, so we made this collapsible igloo for 'is benefit. Neat, eh?"

"Do you live in igloos at home?"

"Nah, we've got nice modern 'ouses now, all mod cons, but Grandpa prefers the old way."

Then Eddie saw a truck beyond the igloo. "So that's what made the tracks."

Rosalyn appeared beside Eddie. "I see you're befriending Eskimos, now. No doubt you'll be rubbing noses soon."

"Oh, hello Ros," said Eddie. "This is, er, sorry, I don't know your name."

"Uiritsaktak. It means 'playful'. And please don't call us Eskimos, miss, we prefer Inuit. And in case you were thinking we always rub noses, that's not true neither. See!" And she kissed Eddie on the lips, just as all the other ramblers joined them.

"Come and take a look inside. Grandpa would love to say 'hello'."

"That would be interesting, but I'm afraid we don't have time."

"Eddie," said Tsubrina, accusingly. "Why did you kiss that Eskimo girl."

Eddie looked uncomfortably from Rosalyn to Tsubrina to Hitomi to Pochette to Uiritsaktak. "I, er…" he began.

Rosalyn giggled at Eddie's discomfort and said, "Since all the women you meet want to tell you what their name means, what about 'Rosalyn'? Would you like to know what that means?"

Eddie, sighed, shrugged and said, "Why not?"

"It means 'pretty, like a rose'".

"Well," said Eddie, "I think that's very appropriate."

Rosalyn beamed, Tsubrina scowled, Hitomi laughed, Pochette put her hands on her hips and Uiritsaktak kissed Eddie on the lips again.

Then Henry called, "Now come on, everyone, we'll have to step on it if we're going to make the train. It goes at five to six, so we've only got forty-five minutes to do nearly two miles." He set off towards the road.

Peggy said, "But what do we do about the farmer?"

Uiritsaktak replied "That's all right, lady. We'll look after 'im. Grandpa's a retired doctor and a shaman too, so 'e knows what to do."

Then Winnie said "And what about his poor dog, waiting for his master who won't be coming back?"

"Don't worry," said the dripping Pandora. "I love dogs. I'll look after it. Goodbye, everyone, and thank you so much for providing me with a fantastic story." She squelched back up the track.

Rosalyn said to Eddie "Come along, U Thant."

"Blimey, mate," said Uiritsaktak. "I wouldn't put up with that."

"U Thant, my dear," explained Rosalyn, "is the United Nations Secretary General. Eddie here has been doing his best to foster international relations with Japan, France, and now Greenland."

"Don't forget me," said Tsubrina. "I'm half Polish."

Rosalyn said, "Oh, how could anyone forget you, Tsubrina."

All the others had gone, and Dan shouted from the road, "Come along, you lot! Hurry, or we'll miss the train."

CHAPTER 8

GOING HOME

Sunday 6th May 1962, 5.56 pm

I

The train was standing at Stonegate station as the ramblers arrived. The guard looked anxiously at his watch, wondering where all the expected ramblers had got to. Dan ran into the station and shouted, "Hold it, we're just coming!"

The guard said, "We should've left by now. I can't hold it much longer."

Some passengers on the train were leaning out of the windows. A man waving an Ian Allan train-spotters' guide said to Dan, "This is disgraceful. The train was on time leaving Hastings but now it's a minute late."

More ramblers piled onto the platform, rushed to the train doors, and scrambled aboard. Dan remained on the platform until everyone had got on, then climbed in himself and shut the door.

The guard was about to blow his whistle and wave his green flag, but then Dan heard, ".....left right, left right....." from the road. It was, of course, Muttley's Marchers. Dan opened the door and yelled "Wait!" at the guard.

"Shut that door!" yelled the guard. The train-spotter tapped his watch and informed his companions that the train was now two minutes late.

Dan rushed to the station entrance, grabbed hold of Muttley's arm and dragged him onto the train, followed by the Marchers.

"Apologies, sah," said the Major. "We can't march any faster, the little one would get left behind."

The guard whistled and waved his flag, and the train moved off at last – three minutes late, as the disgruntled trainspotter noted in his little book. The homeward journey had begun.

II

"Oh my goodness," said Peggy as she found a seat. "I haven't run like that since I was at school."

"Only a year or two ago then," said Eddie.

"Flatterer!" responded Peggy.

Rosalyn looked at Eddie quizzically. "You've come out of your shell very quickly."

"What do you mean by that?"

Winnie said, "What's it like to live in a shell?"

Rosalyn ignored her and continued, "Only last week you seemed to be in mourning. Today you're chatting up all the women you see."

"That's not fair. I am not." Eddie looked down sadly.

Rosalyn bit her lip and said, "Sorry. I shouldn't have said that. I was just teasing."

Eddie smiled and said, "It's okay, I suppose I should be over it by now."

Winnie produced a huge thermos flask from her rucksack. "Anyone for tea?"

"Oh, yes please. How kind," said Peggy.

Henry got up, said, "Excuse me, nature calls," and went off to the toilet. As he opened the door, Oliver entered and there came the sound of raucous singing from the next carriage.

"Four and twenty virgins
Came down from Inverness,
And when they went back home again
There were four and twenty less,
Singing...."

Oliver closed the door.

"What are they singing?" asked Winnie.

"Uh hum," said Dan, uncomfortably. "Best not to know, Winnie."

But Peggy said "Don't be such a prude, Dan. I know that song. Sounds like they're having a whale of a time, whoever they are."

111

Oliver said, "It's that young crowd, the Mudlarks. I've been talking to them. They say they've walked fifteen miles and spent two hours in the pub."

"Good Lord," said Peggy, "they must have run all the way."

"Indeed," scoffed Rosalyn. "One of them ran into Eddie this morning, didn't she Eddie?"

"Well..." started Eddie, uncomfortably.

Dan said "I think they're a breath of fresh air. I'd rather have them than Muttley or the Happy Wanderers."

As Henry returned and opened the door, there came more happy singing.

"The jolly old Marquess of Buckingham,
Stood on the old bridge at Rockingham,
"Watching the stunts..."

Henry closed the door and said, "I say, their songs are a bit close to the mark. I wouldn't go near, if I were you, ladies."

"Oh, really, Henry," said Peggy. "You must think we've spent all our lives in a convent. You may remember I used to go out with a Scottish international rugby player, so I could sing along with them."

"Don't you dare," said Henry.

Oliver said, "They wanted me to squeeze into their compartment, to beat the record, they said. The girls are all sitting on the boys' laps."

Henry said, "And a couple of boys are sitting on girls' laps. Some of those young women are quite well built, I noticed."

"You would," scoffed Peggy.

"What was that song about?" asked Winnie.

Peggy said, "I don't think I've heard that one. Let's go and listen."

But Dan said, "No, we can do better than that. I'm sure we can put on a better show."

"I doubt it," opined Peggy.

"Yes, of course we can," insisted Dan. "Let's see now. Oh, yes, here's a good one:

"Knees up Mother Brown..." he started, then most of the others accompanied him:

*"... Knees up Mother Brown,
Under the table you must go, E-I-E-I-E-I-O.
If I catch you bending, I'll saw your legs right off.
Knees up, knees up, don't get the breeze up,
Knees up Mother Brown.
Oh, oh, what a rotten song,
What a rotten song, what a rotten song.
Oh, oh, what a rotten song, what a rotten singer,
too-oo-oo."*

They applauded themselves and cheered. Joaquín and Hitomi had not the slightest idea what the songs were about, but were enjoying the entertainment, nevertheless.

Then Peggy said, "What's that one that goes: *'My old man's...'"*

Henry butted in:

"My ol' man's a dustman, 'e wears a dustman's 'at...."

"No, not that one," said Peggy. I know, it goes*:*

'My old man said follow the van...", then the others joined in,
And don't dilly-dally on the way.
Off went the van with me 'ome packed in it,
I follered on with my ol' cock linnet,
But I dillied and dallied, dallied and dillied,
Lost the way, and don't know where to roam.
Oh, you can't trust a special like the old-time copper
And I can't find my way 'ome!"

After the cheers and applause had died down, the gaunt man in dark clothes from Party Number Two stood up and said, "I'd like to sing something."

Rosalyn whispered to Eddie, "That's Horace Gravey. We call him 'The Undertaker' because of the way he dresses."

"Oh dear," said Dan. "If you must. What had you in mind?"

"It's a little ditty from Shakespeare's 'Twelfth Night'. I'm sure you'll like it."

Horace took a deep breath and started to intone:

"Come away! Come away, death,
And in sad cypress let me be laid.
Fly away! Fly away, breath,
I am slain…. "

The train whistled and went into a tunnel, and by the time it emerged into Tunbridge Wells Central Station, Horace had flown away – under some duress from Dan, if truth be told.

Rosalyn said to Eddie, "This hasn't been a typical ramble by any means, but will you come again?"

Eddie eyed Rosalyn sternly. "I've been assaulted and insulted, I've been knocked over by a human cannonball, I've even been threatened with a gun, for goodness' sake..."

Rosalyn looked dejected. "Oh. So..."

But Eddie continued, "... and I haven't had so much fun for a long time. And I must admit that for the first time since... you know... I even forgot about Steffie for most of the day. I feel a bit guilty about that. But thank you for dragging me along, Ros. Of course I'll come again."

Rosalyn smiled, but immediately her face clouded over. Tsubrina came up and sat opposite Eddie.

"Hello Eddie," said Tsubrina. "Did you enjoy your walk today? Wasn't it exciting?"

She put her rucksack on the floor, and spent an unnecessarily long time bending over it to undo the straps and remove an apple. She had neglected to make use of the safety-pin that Winnie had so kindly provided, thereby giving Eddie a fine view of the ample bosom that spilled out from the unrepaired cheesecloth shirt.

CHAPTER 9

EDDIE AND STEPHANIE

The small hours of Monday 7th May 1962

Eddie was climbing a long, spiral staircase, which seemed to stretch into eternity. In the stairwell, floating up beside him, was a very pretty woman with golden hair, wearing a diaphanous white gown. It was Eddie's late wife, Stephanie.

"So you've forgotten me," she said, accusingly.

"Of course I haven't. It's just that so many strange things happened, and my mind was distracted."

"And you chatted up every woman you met."

"That's not fair. They were chatting me up."

"You encouraged them."

"I was only being polite."

Stephanie laughed. "It's all right. I don't mind, as long as you don't really forget me."

"How could I forget you. You were perfect, everything I wanted in a woman. I miss you so much."

Stephanie leant on the balustrade and said "Give us a kiss, then!"

Eddie bent to kiss his late wife, but she shot up the stairwell and disappeared. Then he woke up.

CHAPTER 10

THE STAG'S HEAD REVISITED

Tuesday 9th May 1962, 6.15 p.m.
The bar of the Stag's Head pub.

The public bar of the Stag's Head was empty apart from Reuben, the landlord.

The door opened, a man entered, and Reuben said, "Evenin' Bert, the usual?"

"That's roight"

After Reuben had poured a pint of best bitter, Bert said, "Oi 'ear ol' Maandrake snuffed it on Sunday."

"Arr," said Reuben. "It was them raamblers as did it."

Bert was horrified. "What, murdered 'im?"

"Good Lord no! 'Eart attack. Got 'is just deserts, oi reckon."

"Arr," said Bert. He pointed into the adjoining 'snug' bar, where a glass tank containing a pike could be seen among a number of other stuffed, encased creatures.

"That poik's noo, ain't it?"

"Arr," replied Reuben. "Them Eskimos did that."

"Eskimos? What Eskimos?"

"Them as was campin' by Mellow Mere. Didn't you 'ear?"

"No."

"They certainly made a good job of 'n. Weren't jus' the poik, noither. Take a look! It's only temp'ry, till the coroner gets 'ere." Reuben nodded towards the snug, then added thoughtfully "Leave yer glass 'ere."

Bert walked into the snug, came to a sudden halt and gaped in amazement. For there, propped up by a spear, still pointing with one hand and holding his shotgun in the other, stood the embalmed body of Farmer Mandrake.

PART TWO

ANOTHER FIFTY PACES FORWARD

CHAPTER 1

NO CARPET FOR MRS WOOD

Sunday 3rd June 1962

Gomshall and Guildford

I

The excursion to Saxmundham and Aldeburgh on May 20th had passed without incident, much to Dan's relief: more excitement like that experienced on the first trip would give Rose's Railway Rambles a bad name, he thought.

If Rosalyn thought their shared adventure at Mellow Mere would bring her and Eddie closer, she would be disappointed. He retreated into his 'shell' for the next few weeks, explaining that running a travel agency almost single-handed (with occasional help from temporary staff since Stephanie's demise) was mentally exhausting over long hours. Despite which, she helped him with his food shopping, and he reciprocated by having flowers sent to her once a week.

But Eddie assured Rosalyn that he would come today, and they travelled to Waterloo together. The journey from there to Gomshall was somewhat fraught, as there had been an embarrassing altercation between Rosalyn and

Tsubrina. The latter once again tried to lure Eddie onto Party Number Two. The former instructed the latter in no uncertain terms to stop pestering him, and opined that she, Tsubrina, already had enough men in her party to last a lifetime. Tsubrina retorted that it was up to Eddie to decide, wasn't it. And when he said he would definitely be joining Party Number One, she told him to be like that then, and flounced off.

But this unpleasantness had been forgotten by the time the twelve members of Party Number One reached the Tillingbourne Inn for lunch. It was a lovely, sunny morning as they walked across Shere Heath and through Albury Warren, and by the time they reached the pub it had got quite warm. They sat in the garden beside the Tilling Bourne itself, a delightful stream that flows from the slopes of Leith Hill to join the River Wey south of Guildford.

Then Henry came up and said, "Hey folks. There's a dartboard in the public bar. Anyone fancy a game?" Everyone was enthusiastic, except Rosalyn and Eddie, who said they would rather stay outside on such a lovely day. Eddie had already bought drinks for Rosalyn, Winnie and himself, so Rosalyn said she would buy the next round and went inside with the others.

Eddie lay back on the grassy bank by the stream and closed his eyes. He heard the sound of splashing, and was amazed to see someone actually swimming breaststroke towards him. The stream had seemed too shallow to allow such exercise. Amazement turned to consternation when he realised that the swimmer had blonde hair and was none other than Tsubrina.

She rose and walked out of the water. All she was wearing was a thin, pale yellow, buttoned shirt, which reached down to her thighs, and being soaking wet was completely see-through.

"You can't escape me, handsome Eddie," she said, in a deep voice, with no trace of a lisp, and started to rip open the shirt.

As a button pinged onto Eddie's nose, he saw someone else sploshing through the water. It was Rosalyn, wearing the same outfit as Tsubrina. Close behind came Hitomi, the Japanese woman, Pochette from the Mudlarks and Uiritsaktak from Mellow Mere, all similarly attired. They all rose from the water and walked menacingly towards Eddie, ripping their shirts.

Then another swimmer emerged. It was Luke, Tsubrina's father, who stood up on reaching them. He was stark naked.

"Thubweena!" he lisped, in a high-pitched voice. "Thtop that immediately". "And you," he continued, thrusting a fist into Eddie's face, "Thtop mething about with my daughter!"

124

Eddie now perceived another woman approaching, actually walking on the water. She wore a long white robe, with wings and surmounted by a shining halo. It was his late wife, Stephanie.

"Go to Hell!" she yelled, thrusting a trident towards Luke and Tsubrina, who had each sprouted a pair of shiny red horns and a long purple tail. They threw up their arms in terror and swam back across the stream, continued swimming through the mud on the opposite bank, and disappeared, still swimming, into the grassy field beyond.

"You too," shouted Stephanie, thrusting the trident towards the other women, who turned into geese and flew noisily away.

Stephanie said, accusingly, "So, my darling, this is what you get up to now I'm gone. So far, I've counted five very attractive women you're chasing."

"Honestly, Steffie, it's not my fault. They're ganging up on me. And take off those wings! You look ridiculous."

Stephanie laughed, removed the wings and threw them into the water.

"And the halo."

The halo clanged onto a boulder. Then she said, "Don't worry, I'll protect you."

A distant, different female voice said, "Who are you talking to, sleepy head?" And as Stephanie faded away Eddie awoke, with a start, to see Rosalyn putting a pint of beer and a half of cider on a nearby table.

Eddie clambered to his feet and sat at the table. "Thanks," he said. "I must have drifted off."

"Were you dreaming?"

"Yes."

"May I enquire what about?"

Eddie hesitated and sighed. "Er, well… I was dreaming about Stephanie, actually."

Rosalyn pursed her lips and said, "You forgot about her last time."

"Yes, but it's less than a year since she died."

Rosalyn smiled and said, "It's okay. Sorry, I shouldn't tease you about it. Was I in your dream?"

"Yes."

"What about Tsubrina?"

"Yes, you were both swimming in the stream." Eddie laughed. "But she turned into a devil."

"She's a devil, all right. I'd keep well away, if I were you."

"She's much too young for me. Not my type at all." He took a swig of his beer and looked away. Neither he nor Rosalyn were entirely convinced of the truth of that statement.

II

Mrs Maud Wood, of 87 Downs Rise, Guildford, was always losing her spectacles. And her long-suffering husband, George, was as usual given the task of finding them. He had already looked in the customary places: between the sofa cushions, on top of the Radio Times, on the television table, by the telephone – to no avail.

"Hurry up, Wood," said Mrs W, who habitually addressed her husband thus. "The carpet men will be here in a minute."

"I'm doing my best, dear. Where did you last have them?"

"Reading the paper at the kitchen table."

"I'm there now and there's no sign of them."

"Well, try harder!"

Mrs Wood's peremptory manner was the result of long service as a sergeant in the Women's Royal Army Corps. She was, it must be admitted, something of a harridan, and one wonders how she and the easy-going George ever got together. She considered all men to be fools, and her husband as a prime example. Looking out of the front window, she dimly saw two men emerging from behind a parked van.

"Ah, here they are. Yes, it's them all right, they're carrying my new stair carpet." She went to the front door and out into the garden. "Cooee!" she called. "Over here!"

III

Party Number One's afternoon walk ascended St Martha's Hill, where they spent a while admiring the view and exploring the lovely little 'Church on the Hill'. Dan pointed out the commemorative headstone by the eastern gate for the great French actress, Yvonne Arnaud, who had died just a few years earlier.

Then they back-tracked a little and veered northwards to Newlands Corner for tea. After that, it was downhill nearly all the way to Guildford, but their good progress was interrupted when Henry, in the lead, yelped in pain.

"What the bloody hell is that?" He had stubbed his right foot on something hard hidden in long grass, which, on investigation, turned out to be a wooden log.

"Language, Henry!" admonished Rosalyn.

"Someone could injure themselves on that," boomed Percy, coldly observing Henry waggling his sore foot.

"You're telling me!" snorted Henry. "I *have* injured myself on it."

Dan said, "We'd better move it out of the way."

"Well, we can't throw it to one side," said Eddie. "The bushes are too high."

"Then we'll have to carry it out with us," replied Dan. "It's only a little way to the road then we can drop it there. Anyone volunteering to help me?"

Their new Venezuelan friend, Joaquín, stepped forward, dramatically placed his hand on his chest and bowed.

"I, Joaquín Carlos Roca Diaz, will 'elp you," he said, his customary wide and toothy grin running parallel with his broad and bushy black moustache. He was naturally inclined to be helpful, and wanted to impress his new friends. Furthermore, since his first trip, he had bought himself a pair of very smart walking boots.

Dan cleared away the grass covering the log, then he and Joaquín lifted it – with some difficulty, as despite being not much more than two feet long, it was quite heavy. They made slow progress, having to try several different methods of carrying, each one proving more uncomfortable: hands under log, log on shoulders, log under arm. Eventually they reached the road, but had to walk on a little way to find a suitable dropping spot.

Just as they were about to drop it, a woman's voice called "Cooee! Over here!" It was Mrs Maud Wood of 87 Downs Rise, Guildford.

Dan looked at her, bewildered. "You talking to us?"

"Of course! Who else is there? Bring it in immediately!" snapped Mrs W, and went back inside.

Dan looked enquiringly at Henry. "What does she want it for?"

"Beats me. Firewood?"

"Or a stool," said Winnie.

"A work of art?" suggested Rosalyn. "Maybe she's a sculptor."

Joaquín looked from one to the other, uncomprehending.

Mrs Wood returned to the door. "Come along, don't shilly-shally! If you're quick you might get a cup of tea afterwards." Such generosity was untypical, but she was in a relatively good mood, now that her carpet had arrived.

"Are you a sculptor?" asked Dan.

"Good lord no! What a silly question."

"There's something fishy here," whispered Dan to Joaquín, "but we'd better do as she says".

Joaquín, totally bemused, and wondering what fish had to do with it, helped Dan carry the log through the door, while the others stood at the gate, to see what would happen. Mrs W was at the foot of the stairs.

"What now?" enquired Dan.

"Up there, of course," she said, pointing to the staircase. "We took the old one down yesterday. It was infester with moths. My brother has it now." Then she called "Wood!"

"Of course," said Dan, looking at the log.

"I wasn't talking to you," retorted the ex-sergeant. "Wood, haven't you found my spectacles yet?"

"Still looking, dear," came the distant response from her husband.

Now Dan was totally bewildered, but he just shrugged and started up the stairs. "Come on," he said to Joaquín.

"Up ze stairs?" said the incredulous Venezuelan.

"Up... ze... stairs," confirmed Dan.

Mrs W regarded Joaquín with disdain. "He's foreign, isn't he?"

Dan nodded. "From Venezuela."

"Oh dear," said Mrs W, for whom all things foreign were suspicious, and a foreign man beneath contempt.

Slowly but surely, they hauled the log up the stairs, stopping halfway for a rest.

"It's very heavy," gasped Dan.

"Of course it's heavy.," said Mrs Wood. "There's a thick pile."

"Should we put it on that?"

"Surely the pile goes on top." Now Mrs W was having concerns about the efficiency of these men, and was already compiling in her head a letter of complaint to the carpet showroom.

Dan shrugged, and the two men continued their ascent.

Mrs W observed their progress, and when they had reached the top said, "I suppose you'll roll it down from there."

Now Dan was sure the woman was insane, but thought they had better humour her. He said to Joaquín, "She... wants... us... to... roll... it... down."

Joaquín stared open-mouthed. "We roll down ze stairs?"

"Not us," laughed Dan, raising his end of the log. "This."

Mr Wood entered the hallway and said, "Here they are, dear," handing the spectacles to his wife. "They were on a bookshelf. Where's the carpet?"

As the harridan put on her spectacles, the log came crashing down, knocking out several banister support posts. Mrs Wood emitted a fortissimo scream. Mr Wood fell over backwards. Dan hastily descended the staircase, closely followed by poor, stupefied Joaquín.

Mrs Wood picked up a dislodged banister post and advanced menacingly on the two men, just as they dashed out.

IV

Meanwhile, a van had pulled up outside number 87. The driver and his mate got out, went to the back and withdrew a large cylindrical object wrapped in brown paper, presumably the actual stair carpet. The driver said, "Excuse me" to the ramblers at the gate, then he and his mate started up the garden path, carrying the carpet.

A loud rumble and the sound of breaking wood was followed by a woman's scream. Moments later, Dan and Joaquín ran out chased by Mrs Wood brandishing one of the banister posts.

"Wood!" she screamed at her husband. "Call the police!"

At the gate, Dan turned and said, "I assume that cup of tea's out of the question, then."

And as the post-brandishing Mrs W advanced, he said to Party Number One, "No time to explain. Run!"

Mrs W saw the men with the carpet. "And what do you want?"

"It's your carpet, Madam."

But when Madam screamed and raised the post, the men turned, fled back to the van, threw the carpet in the back and drove off at speed.

"Men!" screeched Mrs Wood. "I hate all men!"

V

By the time a police officer had reached 87 Downs Rise and taken a statement, Party Number One was walking up the ramp to Platform 5 at Guildford Station.

A bundle of rags occupying one of the platform seats shifted and groaned as they passed. Peggy asked it, "Are you alright?"

A mop of untidy blonde hair appeared, followed by a tear-streaked face.

Peggy gasped, "Why, Tsubrina, what on earth is the matter? You're wet through."

Tsubrina sobbed, "I stopped for a pee... then I got lost... and fell into a stream."

"But where's the rest of your party?"

"I don't know and I don't care. A man with a tractor gave me a lift... but I had to sit in the cart... and it was full of..." She burst into tears.

Peggy had noticed the somewhat unsavoury odour and put a handkerchief to her nose.

"Oh dear," she said. "You'd better come with me. I'll help you clean up, and you can borrow my jacket." As she led Tsubrina to the ladies' toilet, she said to the others, "Can any of you lend her some dry things?"

Hitomi produced a sweater and Dan offered his waterproof over-trousers.

Winnie got her flask out. "You can have the rest of my tea, it's still quite hot."

"Thank you," said Tsubrina, between sobs. "You're all very kind." Then she saw Eddie, turned hastily away, and the tears flowed again.

Rosalyn smiled at Eddie. "I don't think she'll be troubling you on this journey. Your dream seems to have influenced reality – you can have more like that!"

CHAPTER 2

THE MYSTERIOUS AFFAIR OF
THE HONOURABLE CONCUBINE

Sunday 17th June 1962
Ashurst and Eridge

I

She had not been seen before, this woman, and by the end of the outward journey it had been unanimously agreed that nobody would be the slightest bit sorry if they never saw her again.

Five minutes before the train was due to depart, a white Rolls Royce Silver Shadow limousine drove slowly along the platform, preceded by the stationmaster. The chauffeur alighted and opened the rear door, then a shrill female voice was heard.

"I won't go, I won't!" The vowels were clipped, and the consonants were a cross between cut glass and screeching chalk on a blackboard.

"Oh yes, you will," came a gruff male response, "or you know what will happen."

"Huh!" came the petulant response.

The stationmaster approached Dan and said, "This is a rum do, Mr Rose, but it's orders from on high." He handed an envelope to Dan.

"What's all this about?" asked a bewildered Dan.

"It's all in there," replied the stationmaster, nodding at the envelope.

Dan opened the envelope and extracted a letter, together with fifty pounds in ten pound notes. He read the letter, then laughed. "If it wasn't June, I'd assume this is an April Fool. Surely it's a joke," he said.

"No, it's totally above board," replied the stationmaster. "I checked with my superior this morning."

Dan read the letter again, as if to reassure himself of its contents.

Dear Mr Rose,

This request will seem very unusual, but has been agreed with the Chief Executive of British Railways, of whose board I am a member. The stationmaster will confirm.

My youngest daughter, the Honourable Coralie, has become thoroughly spoiled by the debauched company she keeps, and I am determined that she must change her behaviour. To this end, I have devised a program of corrective measures, starting today with a long and hopefully arduous trek in the countryside.

I am aware that you played a significant role in reconnaissance of the Normandy beaches during the planning of Operation Overlord in 1944, and have great faith in your ability and judgement. I am sure that you will be able to 'give her a hard time', as they say. Naturally, I do not wish her to come to any serious harm, but if she should happen to fall in a puddle or get covered in mud, I would not be too annoyed.

I have also drawn my plan to the attention of some friends in the neighbourhood you are visiting, and it is quite possible that they may contribute in some way.

It is also likely that Coralie may try to cause some inconvenience to you and the members of your group, so I enclose fifty pounds, which I hope will enable you to find a way of compensating everyone. If you feel it necessary to exceed this amount, you will be reimbursed by my chauffeur, Jenson, who will be waiting with the limousine when you return.

You may also telephone Jenson on the above number, should you feel it necessary at any time.

Please do not divulge the reasons for this experiment to anyone else, and rest assured that I shall in no way hold you or your group responsible if things go awry. If it helps to achieve the desired result, I shall be eternally grateful.

Coralie will, of course, be unwilling to participate in this plan, but I have ensured that she will have no choice but to comply.

Yours faithfully
Montmorency Turnstone
Viscount Stokenchurch

A young woman was pushed out of the limousine. Incongruously, she was dressed for hunting: olive-green tweed jacket, pale brown breeches and black leather riding boots. Her long blonde hair, framing a sharp-featured but not unattractive face, was topped by a tweed cloth cap.

Dan stared in amazement, and Coralie screeched, "What are you gawping at, man?"

The chauffeur, Jenson, took her by the arm and led her, struggling, to a carriage door. "Sorry, Miss Coralie, but I'm under orders."

A gruff male voice came from inside the limousine. "Do as you're told, girl, and get on the train!"

Coralie pouted, then held out her hand to the chauffeur, who helped her honourableness onto the train. Dan climbed in afterwards and shut the door.

The ramblers had heard the screechy voice, and now got their first view of the person from whom it had emanated. Their expressions said, "What on earth have we got here?"

Coralie ordered Dan, "You will accompany me to a first-class compartment, where I shall dictate my requirements to you."

"There are no first-class compartments, miss" said Dan.

Coralie's face became an ocean of horror. "But… surely you don't expect me to sit…" Coralie cast her eyes around the assembled ramblers with distaste, then "… *hyah!* I want somewhere private so that I can issue my instructions." There was much tut-tutting and offended murmuring from the ramblers.

Dan said, "There's an empty compartment along the corridor, we can go there." He looked at Henry, shrugged, spread his hands and said, "I'll explain later." Then, to Coralie, "Please follow me, miss."

"It's 'Madam' to you, my man."

When they were seated in the separate compartment, Coralie said to Dan, "I shall now issue my instructions. Do you have a notebook?"

"Yes, it's in my rucksack."

"You should keep it about your person, ready for immediate use if required. Get it at once!"

Dan was offended, but swallowed his pride and returned to the main compartment, to be greeted by a cacophony of voices, among which could be discerned, "What a nerve!" and "Well, I'll be damned!", "Did you ever hear anything like it?" and "Who does she think she is?"

Henry shushed them and said, "Listen Dan! No way are we going to walk with that stuck-up prig. What are you going to do about it?"

Dan said, "Calm down, all of you. I'm afraid I must ask you to trust me, and I'll explain later. I'm not at all sure how this is going to turn out, and there may be some inconvenience, but I can say that your fares will be reimbursed and the drinks are on me at the pub."

At this, a great cheer arose and there was more talking and muttering. When it died down, Dan continued, "Now I must return to find out what her ladyship's instructions are!"

"And the best of luck!" said Peggy.

Dan returned to the honourable lady and sat down. "I'm ready, *madam*," said Dan, with heavy irony, and opened his notebook.

II

Back in the main compartment, the end door opened and in walked Tsubrina. She came to Eddie and said, "Hello Eddie, come and join us in the next carriage. Won't you walk with us this time?"

Rosalyn said, "That's right, he won't. He's coming with us, aren't you Eddie?"

"Of course," said Eddie, and smiled apologetically at Tsubrina.

Peggy said to Tsubrina, "May I enquire who the lady with your father is?"

Tsubrina replied, "She's no lady, she's his bit of *stuff*!" She spat out the last word and sniffed.

"Oh, sorry," said Peggy, "I didn't mean to pry".

"That's alright. And she's called Hermione Jiggs-Botworthy. What a stupid name. Daddy's besotted with her but I can't stand her."

Soon after leaving Oxted, Dan returned to the carriage. All eyes were on him. Peggy asked, "What's happening, Dan?"

"It's unbelievable," spluttered Dan. "She wants her own private leader, who can tell her about the flora and fauna and places of interest, a mud-free route, a four-star restaurant for lunch and a thatched cottage for afternoon tea!"

Henry said, "Surely she's not genuine. Maybe she's been sent by the Other Lot, to wind you up."

'The Other Lot' was how Dan's people referred to the original ramblers' excursions, a much bigger crowd, from which he had broken away to set up his own programme.

"Hmm. Maybe. Hadn't thought of that," he lied. It might be good to foster this idea to hide the truth, for the time being anyway.

"I'm with Henry," droned Percy. "Maybe she's an actress, and the Other Lot hired her to come here and cause trouble."

Peggy said, "Whoever she is, let's humour her. Pretend we think she's the real thing and play along with it. Then we can dunk her in a horse trough or something in revenge."

Dan said, "Well, you won't get the chance, because I've decided to be her private leader, rather than lumber either party with her. I have a little knowledge of flora and fauna and I'll do my best. I can work something out from the map."

Peggy said, "This is very noble of you, Dan. You deserve a medal. If I were you, I'd try to put her off coming again, in a subtle way."

"Such as?"

"Well, walk her along the muddiest paths you can find, with the thickest brambles and tallest stinging nettles."

"Funny you should say that. It's just what I have in mind. You get off at Ashurst, as planned, then I'll continue to Eridge with Her Ladyship." He knew of a low-lying path and some ponds not far from there, and after all last week's rain there should be plenty of opportunities to 'accidentally' dunk Coralie in the mud or water.

"And what about her four-star lunch?"

"Neither party is going to Frant, so I'll take her there. Henry, please buy a round of drinks at lunchtime, then I'll reimburse you later. Have you got enough money?"

Luke had come to see what the fuss was all about. He said, "Give us a fiver," but Tsubrina said, "It's all right Daddy, I've got enough," and Luke glared at her.

Henry said " Between Peggy and me we have, I'm sure. Don't be tempted to lay down your cloak for her, like Sir Walter Raleigh." There was laughter, but everyone was relieved that the Honourable Coralie would not be walking with them.

II

Free of honourable ladies, under the leadership of the ever reliable team of Henry and Peggy Barden, Party Number One had a delightful day, walking to the west of Eridge, with lunch at a superb pub in Withyham.

Meanwhile, the long-suffering, mostly male members of Party Number Two were paying for their seemingly inexplicable loyalty to Luke Trayton, though his mesmerising daughter Tsubrina may have had something to do with that.

This time, though, Luke's 'bit of stuff', the heavily built and heavily made up Hermione Jiggs-Botworthy, provided feminine company for Luke's daughter. Not that it was appreciated. For all her outward skittishness and immodesty, Tsubrina was very lithe and disapproved of unfit women wearing heavy make-up – she didn't need it.

They had made a rather lengthy lunch stop at a pub in Mark Cross, a village to the south of Eridge, where Luke had taken full advantage of a good range of ales, reassured that their cost would be reimbursed.

As usual, ignoring Dan's advice, he had not bothered to check out the route beforehand, so as they were leaving, he consulted his map and, having forgotten where the intended footpath started, asked the barman.

Many older people in this part of the world spoke with a Wealden accent. The barman's was especially thick, but Luke understood him to say that it started next to the post office. Sure enough, almost opposite the pub stood that very building, and Luke assumed that the driveway next to it was the start of the required footpath.

"This way!" he cried and charged along it, walking stick held aloft, followed by his party.

The man in the tartan jacket stopped to take a close look at a discreet little sign beside the driveway. It said, in block capitals, 'HAPPY DAYS CLUB', with 'members only' in smaller letters underneath. Tartan Jacket felt he should call the others back, but they had disappeared around a bend. He shrugged and chased after them.

A few minutes later, at a car park, they found a gate with a sign saying 'Private, members only'. Luke never admitted he was wrong, and would doggedly follow his chosen course until physically prevented from going further.

He said "Ignore that! Landowners often put up misleading signs to keep people out, but it's a public footpath." Then he opened the gate and walked his party along a path between bushes.

They emerged beside a pavilion and a large lawn, where several dozen people lay on towels, enjoying the sunshine. Beyond them were a swimming pool and two tennis courts, all in use. Luke came to a sudden halt and his followers crashed into each other, staring in open-mouthed amazement. They could not help noticing that they were the only people wearing clothes.

The effect on members of Party Number Two was remarkable. Preston Twite ran back and forth along the bush-lined path, repeatedly chanting "Sodom And Gomorrah", Horace Gravey sat on the ground and cried, while the effect on young Oliver of seeing so many naked women is best left to the imagination. Tartan Jacket shook his head sadly, while the other men just stood and gaped. Hermione said "Oh my gawd!" and Tsubrina walked wide-eyed further into the grounds.

A naked man standing on the balcony of the pavilion spotted them and shouted "Intruders!" All activity stopped, and the club members turned to stare at Party Number Two. A few grabbed towels to cover themselves.

The man on the balcony continued, "Where do you think you're going?"

But Luke just fired back a question of his own: "Where's the footpath?"

The man on the balcony said, "There's no footpath. Either you pay the membership fee and undress or get out!"

Some of the male club members advanced threateningly on the ramblers. Luke said "Sorry mate, we'll go quietly," and started back between the bushes.

But the man on the balcony shouted, "Hey, just a minute. It's Hermione Jiggs-Botworthy, isn't it?"

Hermione jumped, looked at the man and asked, "What of it?"

"Don't you recognise me. Archie Haymarket from the drama society."

Hermione took a closer look. "Well I declare, so you are! I never knew you was a nudist."

"I wasn't when we last met. Come on up. Let's talk about old times over a cup of tea."

"I ain't taking my clothes off, nor paying no membership fee either."

"That's alright. I'm the secretary. We'll make an exception."

Hermione climbed the stairs to the balcony, stopped to turn to the ramblers, put her hand to her open mouth in a gesture of mock shock, then waved and disappeared inside the pavilion with the secretary.

Luke glared at them. Tsubrina sniggered and said "Bad luck, Daddy."

The party filed out, except for Tsubrina, who seemed unwilling to leave. She approached a good-looking and rather well-endowed young man and asked "How much is the membership fee?"

But before the man had a chance to reply, Luke dragged his daughter away.

On returning to the road, Luke looked at his map, with no idea where to go. Tartan Jacket tapped him on the shoulder and pointed to a small, factory-like building almost opposite, next to the pub. Along the top of the front wall, in large letters, were the words 'Poe's Toffees', and next to the building was a signpost that said, 'Public footpath'.

III

Poor Dan. The Hon Coralie had done her very best to spoil his day, rasping endless questions about this plant and that. Disappointingly for Dan, the brookside path had been mud-free, and she had taken full advantage of a splendid luncheon with two glasses of fine wine at the pub in Frant.

However, the homeward journey proved a total disaster for everyone. Dan and Coralie arrived back at Eridge station to find an assortment of British Railways maintenance vehicles and an ambulance outside. Party Number One was already there, and its members were standing around jabbering in an agitated manner.

Peggy ran up to Dan and gasped, "We're in trouble, Dan. There's been a derailment just along the track. No trains are running."

"Oh my goodness," said Dan. "Anybody hurt?"

"Seems not. The ambulance is just here as a precaution."

Coralie grabbed Dan by the shoulders and screamed, "Now look what you've done, as if the horrible walk you led me along wasn't bad enough."

"Madam, the walk was not that bad, and you can hardly blame me for a derailment."

"I can and I will. I shall tell Daddy all about it." This did not bother Dan, in fact he was rather pleased that something was going wrong. He felt he had failed to give Coralie the hard time her father wanted. For a moment, he wondered whether this derailment might be the work of one of his lordship's friends in the neighbourhood, but it all seemed very genuine. Surely British Railways would not be persuaded to stage a derailment.

Dan said "I'll have a word with the stationmaster," and strode towards the station building.

The stationmaster said he was trying to check up on alternative transport, but they might have to wait an hour or two. Dan returned to his flock and imparted the news, to a chorus of groans.

Percy, who had been scouting around, bellowed, "It's not all bad news. There's a pub along there, at least we can drown our sorrows while we wait."

So they all trooped into the pub, and there were cheers when Dan said the drinks were on him again.

The landlord was delighted at the unexpected extra trade. "Yer be all refugees from the trains, oi'll be bound," he said.

"That's right," said Henry. "We've been told there'll be no alternative transport for some time."

"Well, while Betsy 'ere serves you oi'll see what oi can do."

Fifteen minutes later the landlord returned, wearing a triumphant expression. "'S all roight," he said. "Moi cousin's looking aafter a coach for a friend, and 'e'll be 'ere in 'arf an hour to take you to Tunbridge Wells. There'll be trains from there. 'E says e'll do it fer five quid, so seein' there's what, fifteen o' yer, that's about seven shillin' each."

Henry said, "I don't see why we should pay extra. If we leave it to British Railways to organise alternative transport, we shouldn't have to pay anything."

Dan replied, "But that could take hours. I suggest we accept this gentleman's kind offer, and I'll pay the cost."

"This is very generous of you, Dan," said Henry, "But why should you have to fork out?"

"Don't worry about it. I have the means, and I'll explain later."

"How much was there with that letter?" asked Peggy. Dan had not said anything about the Viscount's remuneration, but the ever astute Peggy had worked it out for herself.

Dan frowned, then winked and said, "Enough!" He looked at his watch. "But what's happened to Party Number Two? They should be here by now."

"Oh," said the landlord. "Yer didn't tell me there was more comin'. The coach is only small, about twenty seats oi think. Yer'll 'ave to discuss it with moi cousin when 'e gets 'ere."

"Okay," said Dan. "But I'd better phone the chauffeur to say Madam will be late."

Coralie wailed, "This is too awful, I shall miss supper," which was met with laughter and sarcastic cries of "Oh, what a shame!" and worse.

IV

Some forty minutes later, a series of loud bangs announced the arrival of the coach. Everyone went out and surveyed it with dismay. The venerable conveyance had served its country with distinction during World War Two, but the scars were still evident. Few parts of the original exterior remained, and most of the repairs had been repainted in whatever colour was handy, giving it the impression of a patchwork quilt.

Coralie exploded. "I'm not getting into that scrapheap!"

"Well," said Dan, "it's this or nothing."

The driver opened the door and got out. "Well oi'm blowed if it ain't you lot again," he said

Dan said, "Oh yes, I remember you. It's our old friend Stand-in Sid from Spindleford on our first trip. Jolly good of you to come and help."

Sid said, "Oi'm only staandin' in fer moi nephew Jed, who's on 'is 'olidays."

Back in the nineteen-thirties, a well-known psychologist undertook research into why children and some adults stamp their feet when annoyed.

His conclusion was that it was to let off steam when they had no other way of expressing annoyance.

This did not apply to Coralie, who was perfectly capable of expressing annoyance in all sorts of ways. Nevertheless, she stamped her left foot and screamed, "I won't go in that, I won't. I'd rather die!" Then she stamped her right foot. Then for greater emphasis stamped her left foot again, and as if to restore the balance, her right foot once more.

Just then, a long, sleek, black vehicle roared up and, with a screech of brakes, came to a sudden halt behind Sid's coach. It had no windows other than those at the driver's cabin, which were opaque.

Coralie ran up to it and said, "I'm getting on this one."

"But you don't know where it's going, do you," said Dan.

"I don't *kyah*. It must be going somewhere, and anything's better than that dirty old wreck."

A door on the side of the black vehicle slid open and a blinding white light shone out of it. Then two arms shot out of the door, grabbed Coralie and hauled her into the vehicle. The door closed, the engine roared and the vehicle sped off, backwards, the way it had come, around a bend.

The stupefied ramblers stood and stared in amazement. It all happened so quickly, that Dan only then realised that he had let his charge escape.

"Now what do I tell her father?" he said.

"It wasn't your fault, Dan" assured Peggy.

"Good riddance to her," said Percy, followed by a general murmur of agreement. And Dan wondered if this was the work of another of Viscount Turnstone's friends.

While Party Number One boarded the coach, Dan asked Sid, "Can you please wait a few minutes? "We're still a few short."

" 'Ow many more are there?

"Twelve."

"But there's only twenty-two seats, so some of 'em'll 'ave ter staand."

"It's not far, I'm sure we'll manage," said Dan.

The distant noise of a siren grew louder, then a police car sped up and screeched to a halt behind Sid's coach, with a flashing blue light on the roof. The window was wound down and Police Constable Arnold Wheelwright of the East Sussex Constabulary, in the front passenger seat, called out, "Have you seen a black vehicle go past?"

"Why yes, just a few minutes ago," said Dan. "But it didn't go past, it stopped here then went back the way it had come. You must have passed it."

"Didn't see it. You sure it went that way?"

"No doubt about it. Very odd, it was going backwards at speed."

"Dual steering positions, probably," said PC Wheelwright. "Maybe it turned off along that side road back there."

Dan said "What's with the blue light and siren? That's new isn't it?"

"Yes sir, just being tried out. Much better than bells, that's for sure. Sorry, can't stop." To the driver he said, "Quick, Ron, back we go." Ron carried out a smart three-point turn then set off in chase, siren blaring.

Dan phoned Jenson from the pub, and was relieved to find that the chauffeur took the news very calmly, as if he had been expecting something like that.

Then Party Number Two arrived at last. Dan asked Luke angrily, "Where've you been? You'd have missed the train if they'd been running."

Luke said, "Sorry boss, keep your hair on! I got a bit lost 'coz there was a confusing sign."

"We trespassed into a nudist colony," said Tsubrina, with a mischievous smirk. Luke glared at her.

"Did you indeed?" said Dan. "Well, Luke, you've got some explaining to do. But never mind that for now, just get on the coach. It's taking us to Tunbridge Wells, but some of you must stand, I'm afraid."

When Tsubrina got on, she looked for Eddie, who was sitting next to Rosalyn. "I'll sit on your lap," she said, gleefully.

"What a cheek!" exclaimed Rosalyn. "I'm sure Eddie would rather you didn't."

Eddie said, "It's alright, Ros. It's only for a little while."

Rosalyn screwed up her face and looked angrily out of the window. Tsubrina sat on Eddie's lap with a triumphant look, with one arm around his neck. She took full advantage of the situation, leaning closely against Eddie and frequently changing position. This involved a considerable amount of wriggling, which Rosalyn observed with much distaste. Eddie pretended not to notice, but admitted to himself that he was rather enjoying it.

V

On arrival at Tunbridge Wells Central Station, the ramblers' travails were not yet over. As they started to alight, a porter came up with the news that a signal failure at Tonbridge had just put that line out of action too, and London trains were terminating at Sevenoaks. It would be some time before replacement transport could be provided.

"Oh no!" moaned the suffering passengers, with one voice.

"This is becoming a nightmare," said Henry.

Dan said to Sid, imploringly, "Can you please take us on to Sevenoaks? We're stuck otherwise. I'll pay extra, of course."

Sid said, "Oh lor! This is a bit more than oi baargained fer. Oi'll 'ave ter get more petrol now, and it'll cost yer another foive pound. And oi'll 'ave ter phone me missus ter say oi'll be late."

"Well, we've no choice if we want to get home," said Dan. He turned to his party. "Sorry folks." And thought to himself, "Surely this can't be the work of another of his lordship's friends."

Eddie was getting pins and needles with Tsubrina on his lap, but he felt he could put up with it a little longer.

On the way to Sevenoaks, the coach lived up to Coralie's expectations and broke down. Henry, who had some mechanical knowledge, managed to trace the fault and repair it, while the ramblers stretched their legs, and some took the opportunity to relieve themselves in the roadside bushes. But it was nearly ten o'clock by the time they reached Sevenoaks, just in time for the last train to London.

VI

After being hauled into the black vehicle, Coralie had been handed what she was told was an aperitif. Although surprised, she naturally assumed that this was the precursor to supper, and drank it without demur.

She came to an hour or so later, finding herself lying on a couch, wearing nothing but a flimsy and transparent chiffon blouse and baggy trousers of similar material, with a thin veil across her face. Her long, blonde hair hung loose around her shoulders, her feet were bare and a seductive perfume had been liberally sprayed all over.

A similarly attired woman took the dazed Coralie by the hand and led her towards the rear of the vehicle. There, on a couch, reclined a man of Indian appearance, with a luxuriant black moustache, wearing a red robe and a white turban, while a man stood behind waving a large fan.

"Welcome to my harem, my dear," he said. "Come, sit beside me. What is your name?"

Coralie had recovered her senses now, but would have been well advised to remain silent.

"Harem!" she screeched. "Damn your eyes! Never mind my name, what on earth do you think you're doing, taking me prisoner?"

A moment later the vehicle stopped, the door slid open, Coralie was thrown out onto the roadside and the vehicle sped away. She rose slowly to her feet then collapsed onto the grass verge and burst into tears. Fortunately for her, in such flimsy attire, it was a warm evening.

A few minutes later, a police car drove past at speed, then the brakes were slammed on. Its occupants stared back at Coralie in amazement. PC Wheelwright got out and helped her into the back of the car.

Coralie was taken to Tunbridge Wells police station, where she was given a cup of tea and asked to make a statement. The sergeant gave her the only spare coat they had, which was very dirty, having only that day been used during the rescue of a cat from a tree; and the only footwear available, a pair of wellington boots that was much too large for her dainty feet. She was instructed to hand them in at her nearest police station as soon as possible after returning home.

Coralie regarded the garments with disgust, but reluctantly put them on. As the line through Tunbridge Wells was out of action, she was driven to Sevenoaks railway station, where a ticket was bought for her, with instructions to repay when handing in the coat and wellingtons. Then she was put on a London-bound train – the last of the day, as it happened.

Before boarding the train, Coralie gathered the coat around her, and in doing so put her hand on something slimy and wriggly that had crawled out of a pocket. It was a slug. She screamed, tore off the coat, dropped it onto the platform and climbed hastily into the carriage.

One had to feel slightly sorry for the woman. Not only was it the same train that Dan and company were on, but the same carriage. When Coralie recognised her fellow travellers, she tried to hide behind a seat, but it was too late.

Rosalyn said, "I don't believe it! It's her honourable ladyship."

Henry added, "She's a dishonourable ladyship now."

There were gasps and wolf whistles when the see-through nature of her garments became apparent. And there was laughter when the wellingtons were pointed out. But nobody wanted to talk to Coralie, and she refused to talk to them. She was too tired and distraught to do anything more than find a seat in a corner on her own. She tried to hide her face behind the thin veil.

"Poor woman," whispered Peggy. "She looks like a concubine. Whatever's happened to her? I'll lend her my jacket and find out." But Coralie just told Peggy to go away.

Dan had time before the train departed to phone Jenson again, and told Coralie he had done so. She just grunted and curled into the corner. And sure enough, on arrival at Charing Cross, there was the limousine, waiting on the platform.

Dan never managed to establish the truth about the day's extraordinary events. The Viscount's cash did not quite cover his expenses, but he did not bother to ask for more – it was worth it for the experience.

CHAPTER 3

SEE THEM SWALLOWS FLY!

I

Christmas Day, Monday 25 December 1961
A cottage in Sussex

Dan Rose, together with his wife, Alice, and son, Oliver, spent Christmas with his nephew, Jack, and his wife, Daisy, in a pretty little thatched cottage beside the River Line in the charming village of Lindale in Sussex.

Daisy was the secretary to Dominic, second Baron Lindale, who had recently inherited the title, a mostly ruined castle and a considerable fortune from his father, Rodney Pinewood. The ennoblement resulted from Pinewood's efforts during the Second World War, when his sewing machine factory made spare parts for military vehicles.

When Dan mentioned the ramblers' excursions that he was planning for next year, Jack and Daisy were intrigued, being keen walkers themselves.

Daisy asked, "Would you consider including a visit to a castle?"

"I'd never thought of that," replied Dan, "but it would make a welcome change, and a bit of a feather in my cap."

Daisy continued, "Well, the first Baron Lindale imposed a condition in his will that his heirs must allow the public to visit the castle. George doesn't really want to do it, but if he has to, it will be on as few days as possible. I'm in charge of it, so if you like I can fix it for you. How many would there be?"

"Not sure, maybe forty or fifty." Dan frowned. "But we might well have muddy boots. I don't think he'd welcome us in that state."

"Forty's all right, maybe fifty at a pinch. It doesn't matter about mud. Most of the castle was pulled down by Cromwell after the Civil War, and the ruins have a stone floor. The family lives in the part that's been restored, but you won't be allowed in there. And there'll be a cream tea afterwards in the stable block."

Dan hesitated. "What would it cost?"

"There's no charge. It's not worth it just for the odd days when the castle is open. As long as we can demonstrate that the public have been allowed in."

Dan beamed. "Oh well, that settles it then. We can start at Robertsbridge and finish at Battle. I'll get in touch about a date."

"Just one proviso," added Daisy. "You must provide a list of names when you arrive, so that everyone can be checked out again at the end. That's because the ruins will be locked when you've gone and we don't want anyone shut in."

"No problem," said Dan.

II

The Swallow family was notorious in London's Gangland. The late, greatly-feared Stanley Swallow (known as Fingers, due to his dexterity in the noble art of pickpocketing) had been a superb organiser, pulling off a string of successful burglaries, assisted by his offspring, and never getting caught.

But after Fingers died, the family became the subject of ridicule in both criminal and police circles. Without Fingers' guiding hand, their over-ambitious schemes always went awry. Moreover, they were so incompetent that, so far, they had not yet even managed to break any laws in the process. Nevertheless, the local police kept a paternal eye on the family, on the off-chance that they might actually do something arrest-worthy.

Norbert (the eldest, known as Nobby the Job, because he planned the schemes) was quite bright, and tried hard, but no 'chip off the old block' when it came to organising. His siblings, in descending order of age, were Nicholas, alias Knocker Nick (because of his pugilistic nature), William, alias Lardy Bill (over-indulgence in fatty food) and Ethel, alias Teutonic Ethel (considerable strength and leather apparel).

His juniors were something of a liability to Nobby, due to their incompetence. Yet each believed they were capable of working on their own, and only

164

reluctantly accepted Nobby as leader because he alone knew where Stanley's ill-gotten gains were, as the expression goes, 'stashed away'.

One May morning, Knocker, Lardy and Teutonic Ethel were having their usual late breakfast when Nobby (an early riser) came in waving a piece of paper.

"We're going on a ramble," he cried.

"What's a ramble?" enquired Lardy Bill, cramming a whole sausage into his mouth.

"It's a walk in the country," replied Nobby, "admirin' the birds and the bees and the flowers."

""You mus' be jokin'!" scoffed Knocker Nick, slurping a mouthful of very sweet tea, into which he had delivered five teaspoonfuls of sugar.

Lardy cackled. "Yer avin' a larf ain't yer," he opined, prodding his fork into a mound of bacon.

"I wouldn't be seen dead doin' that," said Teutonic Ethel.

"No, listen!" persisted Nobby. "There's one 'ere wot's offerin' free cream tea at Lindale Castle. I read about that place recently. The geezer wot owns it, Baron Lindale, in'erited the title recently, and 'e's got a little daughter."

"So what?" enquired Teutonic Ethel.

"We get into the castle with the ramblers, then we kidnap the little daughter, that's what. Besides, you need the exercise."

165

Knocker spat out his tea, Lardy jerked the bacon onto his nose, and Teutonic Ethel, who had been rocking on the back legs of her chair, fell backwards off it.

"No way!" they cried in unison.

While Ethel regained her seated position, Nobby ploughed on. "Listen! This baron geezer is stinkin' rich, right? So we kidnap 'is darlin' little daughter an' old 'er to ransom."

"An' ow do we do that?" asked Teutonic Ethel.

"I got it all worked aht. We go on this ramble, disguised as ramblers, then we grab 'er, drive off to an 'ide-out nearby, then after a day or two, when the baron's tearin' 'is 'air out, we send the ransom note."

"But we ain't got no car," said Knocker.

"An' we ain't got no 'ide-out either," added Lardy.

"Don't worry," assured Nobby impatiently. "I can organise all that. We've got cousins dahn that way. It's a cinch. This is what we do... "

III

Sunday 1st July 1962
Robertsbridge and Battle

And so it came to pass that fifty-nine ramblers travelled to Robertsbridge and Battle with Rose's Railway Rambles. Most of the usual faces were there, but Dan noted a few unfamiliar ones, no doubt attracted by the visit to Lindale Castle. But he groaned when he found Muttley's Marchers in the next carriage, all in their khaki shirts and shorts and forage caps.

Major Muttley stood and saluted. "Morning, sah!"

"Oh, good morning Major", said Dan, trying to sound pleased. "Were you expecting to join us for the cream tea? Only we're supposed to limit it to fifty and your lot makes fifty-nine."

"No, sah! We have our army rations, so will march to castle and march on spot beside moat while eating 'em."

"Is there a moat?"

"Yes, sah! Checked it out."

Returning to his own carriage, Dan called for attention and said "Listen everybody! Thank you all for coming, no doubt you're all looking forward to the cream tea, but we've been asked to provide a list of names of everyone going into the castle. So my son and assistant, Ollie, will come round for them now. You'll be checked in and out of the castle."

Henry said, "Do they think we'll walk out with the family silver?"

"Of course not!" replied Dan. "It's only so they can check nobody's locked in after we've gone. We'll have the usual parties, Number One with Henry and Peggy and Number Two with Luke and Tsubrina. So tell Ollie who you'll be walking with when he takes your name."

Four people at the end of the carriage looked at each other in alarm. It was the Swallow family, all dressed in outfits that one of Nobby's contacts in the rag trade had provided: assorted anoraks, check shirts, dark blue knee britches, long red socks, army surplus boots and bobble hats.

To his credit, Nobby had done some research into what ramblers wore, one Sunday morning at Victoria Station. It was just unfortunate that it happened to be the Happy Wanderers who turned up. So the Swallows did rather stand out from the others.

Lardy looked decidedly uncomfortable as none of his clothing was large enough for his ample frame. "I feel a right pillock in this gear," he said. "None of the others are dressed like this."

All four Swallows had army surplus rucksacks perched on their laps. Three contained strange cargo for anyone going on a ramble: Knocker's had two bottles of lemonade, several packets of liquorice allsorts and custard cream biscuits, and three recent issues of Bunty, the comic magazine for girls; Lardy's just a length of rope; while Nobby's contained a small bottle of chloroform and a packet of cotton wool. Teutonic Ethel's was enormous, the largest Nobby could find, but far too large for a day trip – and it was empty.

Knocker said, "I don't like this wantin' our names business."

Nobby whispered, "Ssh, keep yer voice dahn! And don't worry, we just give false ones."

Lardy said, "But after we've done the business… "

"Ssh!" interjected Nobby.

Lardy continued in a voice so low as to be almost inaudible, "… and gone off wiv de little girl….."

"Didn't catch that" said Teutonic Ethel.

Lardy settled for a muffled growl. "After we've gone off wiv de little girl, they'll realise we're not there when they check people aht."

Nobby said impatiently and loudly, "What will it matter?" The other three ssh-ed him and he continued in a whisper, behind his hand, "We'll be well away by then an' they'll call the police an' they'll give these ramblers a good goin' over. They'll all be under suspicion."

Lardy whispered, "An' wot abaht saying which party we're goin' wiv?"

Knocker leered and whispered, "Well, I dunno abaht you but I'm goin' wiv dat, what was 'er name, sounded like Sabrina."

Nobby sighed. "It don't matter 'oo we go wiv' as long as we stick togevver and get into the castle."

Meanwhile, across the carriage, and much to Rosalyn's annoyance, Luke and Tsubrina were sitting with her and Eddie.

Eddie whispered to Rosalyn and nodded at the Swallow family across the carriage. "They're a strange lot. Look at the way they're dressed."

Rosalyn agreed. "I reckon this is their first time rambling."

Tsubrina said, "What are you two whispering about?"

"Nothing important, mind your own business," retorted Rosalyn.

"There's no need to be rude, I only asked."

IV

At Robertsbridge Station, Major Muttley led his Marchers off along Station Road: nine of them in single file, with the diminutive one of indeterminate gender trying to keep up at the back.

Dan watched them go with a sigh of relief. As Party Number Two started off, Dan said to his son, who was about to join them, "Just a minute, Ollie, have you got the names list?"

"Yes Dad," said Oliver, producing a crumpled sheet from his pocket. He handed it to Dan and walked quickly away to catch up with the shapely form of Tsubrina at the back of Party Number Two. Normally, she was the only woman in that party but this time Teutonic Ethel had doubled the number.

Dan said, "Okay Henry, we can go now."

As Party Number One set off, with Dan and Peggy at the back, Dan read through the list of names. "This is a bit of a mess. I can hardly make out Ollie's writing." He reached the end of the list. "Uh oh! We've got

170

some jokers: Winston Churchill, Adolf Hitler, George Washington and Judy Garland." He looked at Peggy and raised his eyebrows.

"I'll bet it's those odd four, looked like first-timers," said Peggy. "Or maybe escapees from the Happy Wanderers. Gone with Luke, thank goodness."

"Yes, they did look a bit odd. Could be a bit of a problem when we're checking out, though. They'll just have to remember to respond to the names they've given."

V

Normally, Tsubrina was only too pleased to receive the attentions of the men in her party, but on this occasion she was having trouble with the Swallow family. Especially Knocker, whose attempts to peer down Tsubrina's shirt-front led to her doing up the top two buttons – the first time she had ever done this on a ramble.

Later, when her bottom was pinched, Tsubrina had assumed it was Knocker. But on turning round to slap his face, she was amazed to find a grinning Teutonic Ethel lurking there. All she could do was smile weakly, and when Ethel repeated the assault a little later, Tsubrina just said "Do you mind!" in a shocked voice.

Nobby had seen all this, and grabbed hold of Knocker and Teutonic Ethel. "Cut it out, you two! You're drawin' attention to yerselves."

Knocker laughed and said, "Well, we're only doin' what these uvver blokes would like to do."

"Pretty little thing, ain't she, Knocker?" smirked Ethel.

"An' you keep yer 'ands ter yerself!" retorted Knocker. "I seen yer, grabbin' er bum. Whadder fink yer doin?"

Ethel pouted. "Well, I ain't enjoying this walkin' lark so I might as well 'ave a little bit of innocent fun."

"Innocent!" exclaimed Lardy. "That ain't innocent, it's bloody perverted."

"She likes it," claimed Ethel.

"No she don't!" said Nobby. "You ain't 'ere to satisfy yer perverted tastes. You's 'ere to do a job, jus' remember that."

VI

Party Number One had a grand day. The lunch pub at Sedlescombe did them proud, Eddie was attentive towards Rosalyn, and she felt she was making some progress. The afternoon walk went well as they headed for Lindale Castle.

Party Number Two had lunch at a pub in Netherfield, where the landlady took a shine to Luke.

"I'm so grateful you've brought your group 'ere today," she said, "seein' as 'ow orl moi reg'lars 'ave buggered off to the cricket."

172

Luke said, "No problem, love," drained his glass and banged it on the counter. "Same again!"

"Certainly, and you can 'ave this one on the 'ouse, in gratitude for the business."

"That's very decent of you. Thanks very much." He had already downed three pints of rather strong cider.

Tsubrina gave her father a stern look. "Daddy, don't you think you've had enough already?"

Luke snorted and said huffily, "Stop fussing, girl! It'd be rude to turn down this lady's kind offer." He prided himself on his ability to hold his drink.

Nobby had instructed his gang to have no more than one pint, to keep their heads clear for the job in hand. But when he went to the toilet, his three siblings rushed to the bar, ordered a pint of best bitter each and knocked them back in one long gulp. But Lardy had not quite finished his pint when Nobby returned.

Nobby grabbed Lardy's elbow and growled, "So, soon as me back's turned, you fink you can ignore my instructions." He turned to Knocker and Ethel. "'Ave you two 'ad anuvver one an' all?"

"Oh no, Nobby."

"Oh yes, Nobby, you mean," said Lardy indignantly."

"Snitch!" said Ethel.

"Grass!" added Knocker.

Knocker and Lardy started to fight, but Nobby pulled them apart. "Cut it out! It's just as well these blokes are all droolin' over that Sabrina tart or they'd 'ave noticed us."

Luke finished his cider and shouted, "Time to go. Be outside in five minutes."

VII

Dan called the ramblers together by the castle entrance. "Strange, the drawbridge is up. But we are a little early."

A voice called "Hello Dan." It was his nephew's wife, Daisy, from a window above the gatehouse. "I'm afraid we're not quite ready. We'll be down in about twenty minutes if you don't mind waiting. Why don't you have a look round outside? You can walk round the moat."

Rosalyn said, "I'm disappointed there's no water in the moat. That would look so much nicer."

"But then we'd have to swim round it," said Henry.

Knocker said to Nobby, "'Ave we gotta do that?"

"We jus' stick wiv the ramblers till we gets our chance, remember?"

As the ramblers descended steps by the drawbridge into the moat, a clumping sound could be heard, accompanied by the commanding voice of Major Muttley: "Left, right, left, right….."

174

"Uh oh," said Dan. "Here we go."

"… left, right. Halt!" Major Muttley approached Dan and saluted. "All present and correct, sah! We'll march round moat for a while, then have our rations."

"If you must," said Dan with a sigh. "But please keep your voice down. We don't want to hear you shouting and marching while we're inside."

"No problem, sah! I have range of command styles, for use depending on circumstances. Like this one for when we're attacking but don't want the enemy to hear."

The major called his platoon to attention, then whispered, *fortissimo*, "By the left, quick but quiet, down steps, march! Left, right, left, right…" as they descended into the moat.

A small door some three feet above the moat opened and a tousled mop of light brown hair appeared in the doorway. A child's voice said, "Who'd like to see the dungeon?"

"That's a good idea," said Dan. "It'll fill in the time nicely."

Muttley stopped suddenly. "Halt!" he commanded, and the Marchers crashed into each other on the steps. "By heaven! We'll do that too. Good training to see how prisoners kept in days of yore."

The tousled head dropped into the moat, then dragged a small stepladder out. It was a small girl, about ten years old, in a red-striped teeshirt and blue dungarees. Nobby whispered to his siblings, "That mus' be the little daughter. Keep close to 'er. We'll wait for a chance to nab 'er."

"You can easily get in now," she said, and one-by-one, the ramblers climbed into the dungeon.

Then Major Muttley commanded, "By the left, upwards, march!" and led the Marchers up the ladder.

Nobby whispered to his siblings, "Go on, up yer get! Keep close to the kid, and 'ave the dope and rope 'andy." The Swallows climbed the ladder.

While Dan awaited his turn, at the back, a battered old Landrover pulled up outside the castle gate.

About to enter the dungeon, Nobby whispered to Knocker, "This mus' be our getaway wheels. Cousin Ebenezer's the driver. The idiot, 'e's s'posed to park dahn the road, out of sight."

The driver got out, and Nobby muttered, "That's not Ebenezer. It's Cousin Sid. What's 'e doin' 'ere?"

And Dan said, "Well I never, it's our old friend Stand-in Sid."

Nobby groaned. "Shit! 'E' knows 'im."

Sid said, "Oh lor'. Not you lot again. Oi gets into trouble when you lot turns up."

"I'm sure that's not true," said Dan. "But what are you doing here anyway?"

"Oi'm staandin' in fer moi brother Ebenezer. E's broken 'is leg.""

"And what does he do?"

"E's a … "

But before Sid could say "burglar", Nobby interrupted, "That's a fine old Landrover. What year is it?"

"Oi got no idea," said Sid.

Peggy shouted, "Come on Dan, we're waiting for you. It's jolly cosy in here."

When everybody was inside, the little girl climbed the ladder, pulled the door shut and locked it, then removed the big iron key. Apart from a chink of light from the keyhole, it was completely dark inside.

"Oi," shouted several people.

"What are you playing at, girl?" cried Dan.

"Now you're my prisoners," shouted the girl through the keyhole. "Everybody must pay me a pound to get out." There was much gasping and some laughter.

"Don't be silly!" said Dan. "We're not going to do that. Now open this door immediately."

"Oh," said the girl, disappointed. "How about ten shillings?"

"No!" said Dan. "Now open that door at once!"

Major Muttley shouted, "Permission to break door down, sah!"

"Thank you Major, but that won't be necessary."

The girl continued bartering. "Five shillings?"

"No! Open the door now or I shall tell the baron."

"Oh. Well then, a pound for the lot of you, that's my final offer."

Dan sighed and said, "All right, my dear, I'll give you a pound if you'll open the door."

There was the sound of a key turning, the door opened and the girl stepped inside. "Where's my pound then?"

The sudden daylight revealed that Tsubrina was kissing Eddie passionately on the lips. Rosalyn yelled, "I see! So that's your game," and started to pull Tsubrina away.

Tsubrina shouted, "Go away! He likes it."

"No he doesn't. Do you, Eddie?"

"Well..." started Eddie.

During the daylit period, Henry had noticed another door and opened it. "Look, there's steps going up. Follow me!"

As the ramblers filed out, Nobby motioned his gang towards the outer door. He slammed it shut, there was the sound of a scuffle and a muffled scream.

The steps led up to the castle courtyard, where Daisy was standing by the now open castle gate, with the drawbridge down.

"So there you are," she exclaimed. "I wondered where you'd all got to. What were you doing down there?"

Dan said, "A little girl invited us into the dungeon then locked us in."

"Oh dear, that'll be the baron's daughter, Jemima. She's a little rascal."

"I'll say," said Henry, laughing. "She held us to ransom."

"Did you give her anything?"

"Dan's promised to give her a pound".

"Then you got off lightly. Last time she ordered everyone to take their clothes off, and some had actually started to strip before I rescued them."

VIII

While the ramblers climbed the steps to freedom, the Swallows quietly slipped through the outer door into the moat and made their way to Sid's vehicle. Teutonic Ethel was struggling with her oversized rucksack, now bulging with something that seemed to be moving inside.

"Quick," said Nobby. "Ethel, shove the rucksack in the boot. Gently now! Don't hurt the kid."

They all got in and Nobby ordered Sid to get going, but as they passed the drawbridge, he yelled, "Pull up! There's the kid."

Dan was in the act of giving a pound note to little Jemima.

Teutonic Ethel asked, "Oo's in the boot then?"

"I dunno," said Nobby. Then to Stand-in Sid, "Drive on till we're out of sight, then we'll look."

But as they drove away, Jemima pointed at some birds flying above. "Look! Swallows," she said.

"Oh bloody 'ell!" exclaimed Knocker. "We bin rumbled."

They reached a passing place and pulled in. Nobby and Knocker got out, opened the boot and undid the rucksack straps. A forage cap appeared, then a cherubic face with a bewildered expression. It was the little Marcher of indeterminate gender.

"Where am I?" it said, in a rather high, but certainly not childish voice.

"What is it?" asked Knocker.

"I dunno, but it ain't no little girl," said Nobby.

Lardy and Ethel joined them. "'Ow much could we get for that?" enquired Lardy.

"We'd probably 'ave to pay someone to take it away," said Knocker.

"We'd better do it in," said Ethel, "or it'll shop us."

"Don't be daft," said Nobby. "We don't do murder. They might 'ave already called the rozzers by now anyway. Get it out the rucksack and push it towards the castle. It can make its own way back. Then we clear off sharpish."

The Landrover roared away as the dazed little Marcher staggered back along the drive.

As the ramblers were led through the castle ruins to the stable block for tea, Rosalyn pulled Eddie into a side passage.

"What's the matter?" asked Eddie.

Rosalyn waited till the others had passed then whispered, "You didn't have to let that girl kiss you like that. Why didn't you stop her?"

"Er, well, as a matter of fact, I thought it was you."

"Oh." Rosalyn was silent for a moment, then removed her spectacles. "But this is how I kiss." She threw her arms around Eddie's neck and kissed him full on the mouth for a full ten seconds. It might have continued, but the sound of boots clomping along the cobbles brought an end to their embrace. It was Major Muttley.

He marched up to Dan and said, "Sorry to trouble you, sah, but do you by any chance have our little one amongst your number?"

"No," said Dan. "I'm sure we don't, I'd have noticed."

"Wonder what's happened. Sorry to have interrupted. Better look round outside" The Major saluted, performed an about turn and marched back over the drawbridge, to find the little soldier staggering towards him.

"Ah, there you are, Blenkinsop," he said. "Where did you get to, and why didn't you ask permission to fall out?"

The little one squeaked, "I was taken for a short..."

"Taken short, eh?" interrupted the Major. "Ah well, happens to us all sometimes."

X

As the ramblers went out of the gate, Dan ticked off their names on his list. He turned to Daisy and said, "Four more to go. Thank you so much, we've had a great time and a wonderful tea. It's really kind of His Lordship to treat us. Please thank him for us."

Daisy said, "You've already thanked him, and the Baroness, as you came out of the stables. They were serving. Wave goodbye!" She nodded at the stable.

"Good Lord!" Dan waved back at the noble couple. "Why didn't you introduce us?"

"They didn't want to be identified. They're a lovely, down-to-earth couple, despite their wealth, and don't spend money on hiring staff when they can do a job themselves."

"Well I never, how admirable! Now where are those four? I bet it's the ones who gave false names."

"Oh dear," said Daisy. "This doesn't look good. I hope they haven't hidden themselves away with the idea of carrying out a burglary or something."

"That would be awful after His Lordship's kindness," agreed Dan.

Little Jemima was standing nearby. "It's alright," she said. "I saw four of your people get into a car and drive off. They won't get far, coz I've got these."

She held up a pair of car number plates.

XI

The Landrover was on the main road now.

"What's that noise?" asked Knocker.

"Oh bloody 'ell," moaned Nobby. "Sounds like one of them new police sirens. It's coming from be'ind."

His three siblings in the back looked round.

"There's a blue flashin' light," observed Lardy.

"That'll be it, then," said Nobby. "We're done for."

Sid said, "Oh lor, oi knew oi'd get into trouble. What do oi do now?"

"Just keep calm," said Nobby. "We ain't got nuffink 'ot wiv us."

The police car caught up, flashed them to stop, and an officer approached them.

"We've 'ad it now," said Knocker.

"We should 'ave done in that little wotsit," added Teutonic Ethel.

The officer tapped on the driver's window, and Sid wound it down.

"Sorry to delay you sir," said the officer, "but your vehicle has no number plates. Can you explain?"

The Swallow family glared at Sid, who said "They was there when oi started... oi think."

Nobby said, "You've come at the right time, officer. We were just on the way to the police station to report their theft."

The policeman got out his notebook. "Then I can save you the trouble, sir."

So, once again, the Swallows had failed to commit the crime that Nobby had so carefully planned, and nobody knew except them... and Stand-in Sid, who was family and wouldn't snitch... and the little Marcher, who assumed it had all been part of the training.

CHAPTER 4

HERE WE GO THROUGH THE HOLLY BUSH

Sunday 15th July 1962
Polegate and Eastbourne

I

It was a rotten day for July – blustery, cold and wet – and there was a very poor turnout of just seventeen on the excursion to Polegate and Eastbourne in Sussex.

Both parties started from Eastbourne, walking together as far as St Bede's School. Tsubrina was now resigned to the fact that Eddie would walk with Rosalyn, whatever she tried, but told him she looked forward to seeing him later.

Party Number One, with eight members, was obliged to battle a strong south-westerly headwind across Beachy Head on the way to their lunch stop at the Birling Gap Hotel. Party Number Two, with nine, took an inland route across the Downs, heading for the Tiger Inn at East Dean for lunch.

Both parties were to finish at Polegate, with a tea stop at Jevington. Party Number One's planned afternoon route went through Friston Forest, while Party Number Two followed a circuitous route over the Downs via Willingdon and Coombe Hills.

All went well for Party Number One until, on reaching a little hut in the forest, the ladies (Peggy, Rosalyn, Winnie and Hitomi) requested a toilet stop, and Henry led the gentlemen (himself, Eddie, Dan and Percy) the customary fifty paces forward.

As the ladies returned through the trees, Peggy called the others over. "Look at these pretty little pink flowers. Any idea what they are?"

Rosalyn was quite knowledgeable about flora and exclaimed, "Good heavens, I think they're pyramidal orchids. There's more over there."

"And a little clump here," said Winnie.

Hitomi grew quite excited and said, "Oh, yes, lovely! They are called 'ran' in Japanese. I must take photo." She took off her rucksack and extracted her camera.

They spent several minutes over this, and when they were ready to rejoin the gentlemen, Peggy said, "Which way did we come in?"

"I think it was this way," said Rosalyn.

"No, I'm sure it was that way," said Winnie.

"I'll give 'em a shout," said Peggy. "HALLO!" There was no reply. She tried again, but the only sound was of a power saw whirring in the distance.

"The men must be getting worried," said Rosalyn.

"Henry and I have been in this situation before," said Peggy. "He knows I've got a map and won't worry unless we don't make it back to Polegate in time for the train."

"Eddie might worry," said Rosalyn.

Peggy smiled. "Maybe, but absence makes the heart grow fonder."

Rosalyn blushed and said, "I mean, for all of us." Also, she was well aware that, in her absence, Tsubrina would take full advantage when she met Eddie at the tea stop.

"I'll check my compass," said Peggy. We should be heading north-east. Not that I'm much good with it, I always get confused about what to do about magnetic north."

"Don't you subtract seven degrees or something?" suggested Rosalyn.

"Or is it add seven degrees?" asked Peggy.

"You've lost me completely," said Winnie.

"Well," said Peggy, "I think north-east is that way, roughly." They walked out of the trees and came to a three-way junction.

There is a point in Friston Forest where a number of bridleways converge on several junctions, and it happened that the ladies had chosen to relieve themselves in the middle of this tangle of routes.

Rosalyn said, "So which way now?"

Peggy looked at her map and compass and said, "None of them looks right to me. Oh lord, what to do? Let's give it another go and all shout together."

"HALLO!"

Still no response from the gentlemen, but a woman's voice from the left said, "Hallo there."

Turning towards the voice, their gaze was met by an apparition that seemed to have stepped straight out of a Rudyard Kipling story. It was a short, stout woman dressed overall in khaki: shorts down to her knees and a safari jacket. Dangling from the pith helmet perched precariously on top were a dozen corks. And she was carrying a long pole that rose a foot above her helmet, topped by a carved head and festooned with a veritable mop of coloured ribbons.

"Are you one of Major Muttley's lot?" asked Peggy.

"Never heard of 'im. Was he in Simla?" The voice had a decidedly military bearing. "Hubby was a colonel there, don't yer know. Died in fifty-five. On me own now. Walk a lot. You lorst?"

Peggy said no, Rosalyn said yes. They looked at each other and giggled.

"Well, yes, I'm afraid we are a bit," said Peggy.

"Where you headin'?"

"Jevington."

"But that's where I'm headin'. Know this area like the back of me hand. Wanna come with?"

"If you wouldn't mind."

"Delighted to have some company." The colonel's widow waved the fluttery pole vaguely in the air. "Short cut this way. Follow me!"

Watched in amazement by our quartet, she dived into a clump of holly bushes.

"She crazy," observed Hitomi.

"I'm not going that way," said Winnie.

"Nor me," chorused the others.

"Do you suppose she's going in the right direction?" asked Rosalyn.

"We've nothing else to go on," said Peggy. "That track seems to be closest to the way she went. Let's take it."

II

Back at the little hut, Henry said, "What's taking them so long?" He called out, "Peggy!" If there was a reply, it would have been drowned by a nearby power saw. He tried again, louder. Nothing.

Several minutes later, Eddie said, "I'll go and look." He walked back along the track.

Dan called after him, "Don't look too closely, they may not have finished their business!"

"They must have done by now, unless they're doing number twos!" said Henry.

Eddie returned a few minutes later. "No sign," he said.

"Maybe we should fan out and check the woods in all directions," suggested Percy.

"Good idea," agreed Henry. They set off through the trees in various directions, calling out, but after a further five minutes returned, lady-less.

"This is ridiculous," said Eddie. "They must have finished by now."

"There's a junction over there," said Percy. "I reckon they came out there, then took the wrong route."

Henry said, "It's not like Peggy to get lost, but she's got a map, so they'll be okay. Let's press on, I'm sure we'll find them at Jevington."

Eddie said, "I don't like leaving without them."

"What else can we do?" asked Henry. "We can't just wait here."

"Don't worry, Eddie," said Dan. "Rosalyn's in good hands. She'll be alright."

Eddie looked at Dan reproachfully. "It's not just Rosalyn. I'm concerned for all of them."

Dan just smiled and walked on.

III

In ten minutes, the three women reached another junction.

Peggy consulted her map and compass again. "This still doesn't match up with anything on the map, as far as I can see. I think there must be something wrong with this compass. Look, there's a big bubble in the liquid, that's not good. I wonder…"

She was interrupted by several loud expletives from up to their left. The long pole with multicoloured tassels flew through the air and landed on the track. Then the head of the colonel's widow appeared out of a bush. She seemed to be caught, but with a great effort freed herself, only to fall over and roll down an embankment onto the track. She stood up, facing away from our women, and shouted into the bushes. "This way! You still there?"

"We're here," said Peggy. "Are you alright?"

The widow wheeled round. "Aha! So you are. How d'yer get there? Keep going! Same direction." She stamped her way through a patch of bracken and headed down a steep slope. There was the crack of a breaking branch, then "Whoooaaah!" followed by more breaking branches.

"Take care!" shouted the widow. "It's not too bad once you're past the drop. Mind the badger hole."

The ladies watched in horror, then Peggy giggled and said, "Yes, well, I think we'll have to follow our noses. If the sun was out, we could check our bearing from it."

"I think sun is that way," said Hitomi. "Look, is faint bright light behind cloud."

"Yes, indeed there is. Well done, Hitomi." Peggy looked at her watch. "It's three-thirty-five, so the sun should be in the south-west now, which means that Jevington should be over there. And wouldn't you know it, none of these tracks goes that way. We'd better go right then turn right again at the first opportunity."

"At least it's downhill," said Winnie.

Some minutes later. they reached a sunken track and followed it out of the forest and down to a lane.

Looking right, Peggy said, "Ah, there's a church spire. I hope it's Jevington, in which case we should be in time for tea."

As they walked down the lane, Winnie called out, "Look, there's that madwoman."

The military widow was standing in an adjacent field, brandishing her pole at a herd of cattle. Most of them ran off, but standing its ground was an enormous bull, clearly unimpressed. It advanced a few paces and bellowed. The widow retreated a few paces. The bull stopped. The widow stopped. Then she advanced a few paces and banged her pole on the ground three times. The bull lowered its head and pawed the ground three times. The widow retreated a few paces. The bull advanced a few paces.

"They are dancing," said Hitomi.

Suddenly the bull charged, the widow turned and ran, then disappeared.

Rosalyn gasped. "Where is she?"

"I hope she's not under the bull," said Winnie.

But the widow emerged from a ditch, dripping wet, with the bull now on the far side of the ditch. Thus emboldened, she waved her pole triumphantly at it. But the bull found a crossing point and resumed its charge, further enraged by the insolent behaviour of its target.

The widow ran and scrambled up an embankment on the far side of the field. She ran a little way along the top of it then turned to see the bull following. She jumped, and there was a splash. Beyond the bank lay the Cuckmere River. The bull stopped, snorted and returned to the field. No further effort was necessary, he had won.

IV

If Peggy had consulted her map, she would have realised that the church they saw was not St Andrew's at Jevington, which has a tower, but St Catherine's at Litlington, which has a spire. The symbols on the map are quite different. However, the famous tea garden at Litlington was open, and our women refreshed themselves there.

Meanwhile, the four men from Party Number One reached the Eight Bells pub in Jevington, which had agreed to provide afternoon tea for all the ramblers. However, the landlord was annoyed, as Dan had said there should be about forty people. He had

193

telephoned that morning from Eastbourne to say they were just seventeen, due to the awful weather, but now, minus the four women, they were down to thirteen.

Too much food had been ordered, and not all of it would keep. The ramblers did their best, cramming themselves with cake, scones, jam and cream, excellent value for eight shillings and sixpence. And Dan paid a little bit extra on the side to keep the landlord happy.

Party Number Two had arrived first, and Tsubrina's face lit up when the four men of Party Number One entered.

"Where's your lady friend?" she enquired of Eddie.

"We've lost all our ladies," replied Eddie. "They must have taken a wrong turning in the forest."

"So I've got you to myself at last."

"Well..." started Eddie.

Dan intervened. "Now stop teasing him, Tsubrina."

Tsubrina pouted. "Just a bit of fun, Mister Rose. I'm sure Eddie can take care of himself."

Eddie excused himself to visit the toilet. Looking in the mirror, he imagined that Stephanie, his late wife, was standing beside him.

"What should I do, Steffie? I'm fond of Rosalyn, and Tsubrina is very sweet, in a strange sort of way, but I don't want to get too involved with either of them. I can't forget you."

"You don't have to forget me, silly boy! Just be pleasant to them and let nature take its course. I'll still be here when you need me."

Dan came in and said, "Who were you talking to?"

"I... er... I was just muttering to myself about the lack of soap. We should complain to the landlord."

"We'll do no such thing! We're already in his black book because of the low turnout."

"Oh, all right," said Eddie meekly.

"Peggy phoned just now," said Dan. "They got lost and ended up in Litlington, so they're having tea there and will see us on the train at Berwick."

"Thank goodness for that," said Eddie.

V

The two parties (to be precise, one-and-a-half parties now) walked together from Jevington to Polegate. Henry and Luke argued about who should lead, but Dan said, "Stop quarrelling, you two. I'll lead for a change. Eddie, would you like to be rearguard? It'll be good experience for you. I'm sure Tsubrina won't mind."

"That's all right, Mr Rose," she replied. "I'll walk with him and teach him what a rearguard has to do."

It will come as no surprise that Tsubrina took full advantage of the situation. Soon after setting off, she took Eddie's hand, which embarrassed him rather, but he decided it would be rude to let go. They walked hand-in-hand for a while, then on reaching a field gate, which lay a few feet back from the path, Tsubrina pulled Eddie to the gate, pressed him against it and kissed him full on the mouth. Taken by surprise, Eddie let it happen, but then imagined he saw Stephanie, sitting on the gate and wagging a finger. "Make up your mind, do I get involved or not?" he thought, and pushed Tsubrina away.

"What's the matter?" she said, frowning. "Don't you find me attractive?"

"Yes, damn it, I do, but..."

"Are you in love with that woman?" Tsubrina looked downcast.

"I assume you mean Rosalyn. No, I'm not in love with her."

"What, then?"

"It's difficult to explain," said Eddie quietly, then smiled. "Come on, we'd better get a move on or they'll wonder where we are."

They walked on in awkward silence, then Eddie took a deep breath and said, "Tsubrina, you're very sweet and I do find you very attractive, but the fact is... as I've already told you, I lost my wife last year, and I still miss her very much."

"Oh." She took his arm and said, "It's alright, I understand. I'm really sorry I did that." But she was thrilled by what Eddie had said. Time will heal, she thought.

They walked a little further in silence, then Eddie stopped and said, "Besides, I'm much too old for you. I'm thirty-four, and I guess you're what, twenty?"

"Nineteen. And you're not too old. I like older men, they're more considerate and experienced."

Eddie stared at the ground, then said, "Come on, we must catch up or they'll think we've got lost, and they'll talk, and your father will get annoyed. And poor Dan can't afford to lose any more people."

CHAPTER 5

PERCY THE VAMPIRE

Sunday 29th July 1962
High Rocks and Hartfield

I

Percy Fordingbridge – he of the booming voice and lugubrious expression – was very tall (six foot three) and lanky. The usual rainwear on offer in outdoor equipment shops was too short for him, so he had acquired a long, black poncho, a wrap-around waterproof garment adapted from the blanket that is worn by many of the indigenous people of South and Central America.

One rainy July Sunday, on a poorly-attended excursion to High Rocks and Hartfield in Sussex, wearing the above-mentioned garment, Percy stopped to relieve himself in the bushes, unnoticed by Peggy, the rearguard. He ought really to have told her, but was too embarrassed, having stopped once already. She would then have stopped at the junction, where Party Number One turned left, to make sure he was following. Instead, he plodded straight on, and on, and on. The path, which had been quite clear, became ever narrower, and eventually petered out.

"Oh bugger!" Although alone, Percy said this in his usual loud voice, and a pair of greater spotted woodpeckers that had been exchanging taps among the nearby oak trees stopped their conversation.

"Anybody about?" he boomed. There came no response.

Ramblers who become lost are advised to retrace their steps to the last known position then start again. But as he had no map, and no idea where he was, such action would have had no benefit for Percy. So he just kept going in the same direction, thrashing through bracken, nettles and bushes, until he became thoroughly disorientated and disheartened.

"Bugger!" he yelled. Then again, "Bugger!" for effect. His vocabulary of oaths was rather limited. The woodpeckers glared at him indignantly and flew away to resume their conversation in a quieter location.

Percy eventually reached a precipice by a drop of some thirty feet. It was a disused sandstone quarry, part of a geological feature known as the Tunbridge Wells Sand Formation.

"Now what do I do?" he enquired of a nearby hawthorn bush. "I can't jump, I'd break a leg at the very least." Access to left and right from his lofty location was blocked by dense brambles and hawthorn.

"Oh Lord! I'm in a right pickle now," Percy informed the bush. "I suppose I'll just have to go back the way I came."

He sat down for a rest, with his long legs dangling over the edge of the precipice, and cast his eyes around the quarry. There was a track running past it.

"If only I could reach that track. Bound to lead somewhere."

Looking around, he noticed a tall Scots pine tree to his left, at the side of the quarry. "That's a fine specimen of *Pinus sylvestris*," he mused, and resumed his overview of the area.

Then, after a few moments, he jerked his attention back to the pine. "Hang on! Those branches extend over the precipice. Maybe I could climb down the tree and reach the track."

He rose and edged pinewards along the precipice. But the vegetation almost reached the edge, and he had to push past bushes and brambles. With just a few yards to go, he lost his footing and started to slide down, but on the very point of falling managed to grab a stout root and haul himself back up.

Eventually he reached the tree, took hold of a branch and gingerly worked his way along it, hand over hand. He made good progress for half a minute, but then a loud crack was accompanied by the partial breaking of the branch, and he started to fall. It was the poncho that saved him from severe harm, becoming entangled in the branches.

After a few moments of dazed realisation that he had been rather lucky, Percy tried to continue his downward progress, but the poncho was firmly caught, and he was unable to move in any direction.

"Oh bugger!" he boomed. "Bugger! Bugger! Bugger!"

II

Party Number One had reached the road at the edge of the wood, where Henry stopped and said, "The pub's only a mile and a half away now, but we'll have a ten minute break here.

When rearguard Peggy caught up, he said, "Where's Percy?" Then, "What have you done with him, Peggy?"

"I haven't done anything with him. I thought he was ahead of me."

"PERCY!" yelled Henry. Then they all shouted together. Henry went back along the path, but of course there was no sign of him.

"He probably stopped for a pee, then got lost," said Dan. "He'll be alright, I'm sure. He's got the itinerary, so he'll know we're going to Groombridge for lunch."

Rosalyn was more concerned and said, "But he probably hasn't got a map, and wouldn't be able to read it anyway, as he told us a while ago. What if he doesn't turn up there?"

"Then he'll know we're returning from Hartfield and make his way there."

"But the same thing applies," persisted Rosalyn.

"He's got a tongue in his head. He can ask someone," said Henry.

Peggy joined in. "But he might have hurt himself and be lying somewhere, unable to move."

"Well, let's go on to the pub, then if he doesn't turn up we can call the police from there."

But Percy failed to arrive, of course, and it rather spoiled their lunch. Despite (or perhaps because of) Percy's oddness, the ramblers were quite fond of him.

"All right," sighed Dan. "I'll call the police. But we ought really to do our best to find him ourselves, not just leave it to the police. Peggy, would you please carry on to Hartfield with the party. Henry, come with me, please. We'll go back and search for him. We've both got maps, so we can split up if necessary. Has anyone else got a map?"

"I have," said Rosalyn, "but I don't fancy wandering around the woods on my own."

"I'll come with you," said Eddie, much to Rosalyn's pleasure.

Joaquín stood up, dramatically placed his hand on his chest and said grandly, "I, Joaquín Carlos Roca Diaz, will 'elp also."

But Dan said, "Sorry Whacking. Much appreciated, but you have no map, so I don't think you'd be much help this time."

The Venezuelan sighed and sat down. "No," he said sadly. "I think you are right."

And so it was that a much depleted Party Number One, consisting of Peggy, Winnie, Hitomi and Joaquín, continued along the planned afternoon route.

Dan telephoned the police station at Crowborough from the pub. "His name is Percy Fordingbridge," he told the duty sergeant, Ernest Withers. "He's very tall, well over six feet, and thin, with long khaki shorts. Curly brown hair, glasses. Wearing a black poncho. You can't miss him."

"Well, you've missed him, sir," chuckled Sergeant Withers, picking up a missing persons form. "It's fortunate for you that it's quiet here today, so we might be able to help. And what's a poncho?"

"It's like a big cape."

"Thank you sir. Now where did you last see him, and would you spell his name please?" On completion of the form, the sergeant asked Dan to let them know if they found Percy, replaced the receiver and turned to Police Constable Harry Viney.

"Harry, drive out towards Groombridge and go round the lanes." Handing PC Viney the form, he continued, "Keep a lookout for this character. He's been lost by a party of careless ramblers."

"Okay Sarge. I could call on Danny Haywain on the way. He's the special constable at Groombridge, so should know the area well. He can cycle around and get to places the car can't."

III

Maisie Crimble had been 'stepping out' (as her mother called it) with Danny Haywain's brother, Teddy, for several months. After lunch with Maisie's parents, Teddy suggested that they should go for a little stroll to the old quarry, now the rain had stopped.

"Good idea," said Mr Crimble, "Then we can watch the telly in peace." He winked at his wife.

Half an hour later, on reaching the quarry, Maisie said she needed a little rest, so Teddy, being a gentleman, removed his jacket and laid it on the ground beneath a tall pine tree. They sat down and Teddy put his arm around his beloved's shoulders.

"Oh Maisie," he said. "I do love you."

"I love you too, Teddy," said Maisie.

Teddy gently pulled Maisie back so that they were now lying on their backs.

"Oh Maisie," said Teddy.

"Oh Teddy," said Maisie.

"Oh Maisie."

"Oh Teddy."

Their lips came slowly closer. Then, just as they were about to make contact, Percy coughed and Maisie emitted a piercing scream.

"It's alright," said Teddy. "I'm not going to hurt you."

Maisie pointed upwards. "There's... there's... a monster up there. It's huge, and black, and it's got a horrible face."

Percy's poncho had spread out to resemble enormous black wings, while his face — never of the healthiest complexion — had taken on a deathly hue in the overcast light.

Teddy looked up. "Oh my giddy aunt!" he gasped. "It's a vampire!" He pulled Maisie to her feet. "Come on, we'd better tell Danny." And they ran as fast as Maisie's high heels would allow.

"Oi!" yelled Percy. "Come back! Help!"

IV

Setting off to search for the missing person, Special Constable Danny Haywain was wheeling his bike out of the family cottage in Groombridge, when brother Teddy ran up, dragging a limping Maisie, who had lost a heel from one shoe.

"There's a vampire in the tree in the old quarry," he gasped.

"Don't be daft! You've spent too long in the Crown, I'll be bound."

"We ain't been there," protested Teddy.

"It's true," said Maisie. "It was awful. It was twenty… no thirty feet wide, and had huge fangs, and horns, and blood dripping' out of its mouth."

"You bin watchin' too many 'orror movies, young Maisie Crimble. You always was fanciful."

"I tell you, there's somethin' there," insisted Teddy, "and it ain't nice."

"Alright, alright," sighed Danny, "I'll go an' 'ave a look."

"Oh, Danny, don't go on your own," pleaded Maisie. "It'll bite your neck."

"Don't be daft. It's probably an old parachute or somethin' got caught in the tree. Anyway, I got to look for a missin' person, so I might as well start there." And Danny cycled off.

Five minutes later, arriving at the quarry, he was amazed to find that there was, indeed, a large black shape in the tree. And it contained a face. He pulled out his notebook, in which he had written details of the missing person.

"Are you… " he began, squinting at the missing person's name, but his writing was far from copperplate. "… Pansy Fishingpole?"

The acrobatic Fordingbridge family was poor, but they were honest, and Percy had inherited this trait.

"No," he replied.

"Oh. Sorry to have troubled you then," said Danny. And with that, he cycled back down the track to continue his search elsewhere.

"Oi!" yelled Percy. "Come back! Help!" After a few more buggers, he confided to the tree trunk, "Suppose I'll die here now."

Some carrion crows flew in to roost on Percy's tree. "Oh lord! The vultures are here already," he informed the Scots pine, miserably. "I'll just be a skeleton soon."

V

On returning to the wood, the search party split up. Dan and Henry took separate paths deeper into the trees, while Rosalyn and Eddie followed a broad track that skirted the edge, yelling 'Percy' at intervals. They passed several crags of the Tunbridge Wells Sand Formation, one of which was being climbed by two young men. No, they had not seen Percy.

Half a mile further on, Rosalyn and Eddie reached a disused quarry.

"Let's have a rest," said Rosalyn. They sat down on a metal contraption under a tall pine tree, and she leant against Eddie's shoulder.

"It's turning out to be a nice afternoon," said Rosalyn. "Look, there's a big patch of blue... Oooh!"

"What?"

"Up there. It's... Percy!"

Poor Percy. His fears of being eaten alive by vultures had receded, but he had to wait another hour before the fire brigade arrived and another thirty minutes before they could extricate him from the tangle of branches.

Rosalyn and Eddie waited for him at the Crimbles' cottage, and were given tea and cake. They let Dan know, via the police communication system, that Percy had been found alive and as well as could be expected in the circumstances.

Against all police regulations, Constable Viney drove the three of them to the Anchor Inn at Hartfield, where the remainder of Party Number One had waited, missing the scheduled homeward train, anxious for news of Percy. They were all pleased to see him safe and well, apart from a few minor abrasions, and a badly torn poncho, but Dan was furious.

"You must always tell the rearguard if you stop for any reason," he said. "And I suggest you learn to read a map."

Peggy and Rosalyn leapt to Percy's defence.

"Oh, come off it, Dan" said Peggy. "Alright, he should have told me, but you know Percy will never get the hang of map-reading."

Rosalyn added, "Personally, I'd rather have Percy causing problems than no Percy at all."

The former missing person was mightily embarrassed by this. He shuffled his huge boots around for a while, then said "I'm really sorry for the trouble I've caused. And I'm so grateful to you all for helping and waiting for me. But Peggy's right. I'd never learn to read a map. I've tried and it's just not my thing."

Then, considering he had never done such a thing before, Percy made the following amazing statement: "Before we go home, I'll buy a round of drinks to celebrate my deliverance from the vultures."

CHAPTER 6

RETURN OF THE CONCUBINE

Sunday 12th August 1962
Pangbourne and Goring & Streatley

I

Having gone down with a very bad cold, Rosalyn could not attend the trip to Goring & Streatley on 12th August, and Eddie had to miss it due to work commitments. However, it was some consolation that he looked in each evening to check on her well-being, brought chocolates and flowers, and provided a hot toddy. This concoction of hot water, whisky and honey certainly made her feel better and helped her sleep.

They missed a treat. Just a few minutes before the train was due to depart, Dan and Henry watched aghast as a white limousine drove slowly along the platform, preceded by the stationmaster.

"Oh no, not her again!" they chorused, remembering the occasion back in June, when the Honourable Coralie Turnstone had done her very best to spoil Dan's day, and was spectacularly punished for it.

The stationmaster approached Dan and said "Good morning, Mr Rose. I understand you're already aware of the position Viscount Stokenchurch holds with British Railways, and that you're already acquainted with his daughter, the Honourable Coralie Turnstone."

"Indeed I am. I shall never forget it. But what on earth is she up to now?"

"The honourable lady will explain herself," replied the stationmaster.

Jenson, the chauffeur, opened a rear door, and out stepped the lady herself, though Dan and Henry had to look hard to recognise her as the same person. Instead of the ridiculously inappropriate hunting outfit of the last time, she wore a dark green blouse, blue jeans and rather scruffy walking shoes, which bore traces of mud. Her long, blonde hair had been cut to shoulder-length.

"Hello Dan," she said, then turned to Henry. "Sorry, I don't know your name." Though her accent still betrayed a public school education, her voice had lost its screech.

After a brief hesitation, Dan stammered "This, er, this is my good friend, Mr Henry Barden."

"Pleased to meet you Henry," said Coralie, and shook the surprised Henry's hand.

"Likewise, I'm sure."

"I know what you're thinking," she continued. "I've come to apologise for my outrageous behaviour last time. And to thank you for putting up with it."

"Well, that's very good of you," said Dan. "Apology accepted."

Coralie said "If you'll allow me, I'd like to explain to you and your friends what led to the situation, and what has happened since."

"I'm sure everyone will be absolutely fascinated," said Dan. But the train's about to leave, so let's get on."

As Coralie boarded, there were curious glances from everyone. Then Peggy recognised her face and whispered to Winnie "Good lord! I do believe it's that dreadful woman who was forced on us a couple of months ago."

Dan said to Coralie "Pardon my ignorance, but how should we address you?"

The honourable lady laughed and said, "By my name of course! Coralie is fine."

Dan called for silence, then said "Listen everyone! Most of you will remember that extraordinary trip to Ashurst and Eridge in June, when we had a rather extended homeward journey. And this lady, Coralie, apparently had a very strange adventure. Now she would like to tell us the whole story. The journey takes an hour and a quarter, so it will help pass the time. Ollie, let Coralie sit there and everyone gather round."

Somehow, all the ramblers in the carriage were able to get close enough to hear the story: some sitting, some kneeling or standing on the backing seats and some standing in the aisle.

Peggy asked "Could you please start by telling us what went on in that black bus?"

Coralie frowned and paused. "I won't go into details about that... yet," she said, "but on reflection I only had myself to blame for what happened. I'm thinking of writing a memoir about all this, then you'll be able to read the whole story."

Then she launched into her truly incredible tale, and though her voice was more melodious than previously, she was still capable of talking loudly enough to be heard by all.

II

Dan, I think you already know that my father is Viscount Stokenchurch. I'm the youngest of three children – the other two are boys. They've made a success of their lives, at university and in sport – both have been capped – and are now involved in scientific research.

However, I was the black sheep of the family. I'm neither brainy nor sporty, and knowing I could never match my brothers' success, took to hunting, which was easy to do in view of my family ties.

Yes, I can tell from your reaction that hunting is frowned on by many, and I'm sorry to say that the hunting community in general takes a rather condescending and sometimes hostile attitude towards ramblers. But whatever you may think of blood sports, most of the members of my local hunt are lovely people.

Unfortunately, there was a younger element who went a bit wild and gave the hunt a bad name, and I fell in with them. We would have far too much alcohol beforehand – even in the morning – and make a nuisance of ourselves and ignore the master's instructions.

Eventually we were thrown out of the hunt, but decided to stay together and do our own thing. We called ourselves the Ridgeway Raiders and would ride through crops, along footpaths, crash through farmyards, hold up traffic. Inevitably, we got into trouble with the police, and it was only through the intercession of my father that we escaped punishment, on the understanding that each family would take steps to bring their errant members into line.

To be honest, I feel my father went well over the top with what he called 'a programme of corrective measures', but I must admit that it seems to have worked.

Some of you were present on the first of those measures, and I must apologise for my appalling behaviour, especially to Dan. I still don't understand how, or if, Daddy managed to organise the events of that day, but I cried all night, and even entertained thoughts of murdering him the very next day.

Fortunately, I didn't get the chance, as the next stage of my journey of correction started early the following morning. I was driven to Southampton and told I was to help crew a yacht on a delivery voyage to Iceland. It was really hard work, and I had to comply if I wanted to eat.

Halfway, while I was sleeping, I was woken up and put ashore on St Kilda, where I stayed for three days in a very primitive stone cottage, stuffing gannet feathers into sacks. A woman came in every morning, to leave some very basic cold food, fill a tin tub with cold water and empty the potty. She was very apologetic about it, but said it was for my own good, and slipped a bar of chocolate in with the daily rations.

A fishing boat took me from St Kilda to the Faroe Islands. For another three days I was put up in a village where the dreadful practice is to drive pilot whales into a bay then slaughter them for their meat and oil. Although the local people were very kind to me, the smell was dreadful. I was absolutely disgusted and dreamed of driving my father into a bay and slaughtering him.

Then I was put on board a Danish research vessel and taken to the Norwegian Island of Jan Mayen, which I had never heard of. It lies between Greenland and Norway. There was a visiting team of gravel diggers, and I was told to cook for them. I'd never had to cook before, but to my surprise I found that the basics came naturally to me, I'm actually rather good at it, and the men were appreciative. They were very strong and rugged, so actually I didn't mind this too much. Being so far north, it stayed light nearly all night, and one evening we climbed the island's extinct volcano and had a picnic on the rim of its crater. *[Author's note – that volcano, the Beerenberg, has since erupted twice!]*

I was on Jan Mayen for four days, then a Norwegian air force plane flew me to Bodø in northern Norway. I was kitted out with walking gear and taken on a four-day hike in the mountains, staying in huts. It couldn't have been planned by my father, at least I hope not, but on the last day I slipped on some loose rocks and hit my head on a boulder. I was quite badly hurt and spent two days in hospital.

Even then, my father wasn't finished with me yet. I was flown to Bergen and on to Glasgow, where I had to work at a sewage farm, and I was even taken down a sewer, which was appalling, but the people were very kind to me. I could say I followed the sewage through to the end, as on my last day there I joined its final journey on the steamship Shieldhall, which carries it out to be dumped into the Clyde estuary.

I suppose Daddy had run out of ideas, because he sent our chauffeur, Jenson, to collect me from Glasgow in the Rolls Royce, with a very necessary change of clothes. Despite all the discomfort and hardship, it had been very educational. And corrective, it seems, because I realised how kind most people are, and had learned my lesson.

But it was only on the journey back home that something happened to change my life, which I'm sure hadn't been in Daddy's plan at all. Or maybe it was, on reflection, he can be so devious! And I'd like to mention that my change of attitude was shown by my sitting next to the lovely Jenson, rather than in the back, and I was able to recount my adventures to him.

Anyway, Jenson had brought a picnic hamper, and we stopped halfway for lunch. Just as we were pulling away, I happened to catch sight of a sign saying 'Donkey Sanctuary'. I love horses, and asked Jenson to turn off. I lost my heart to those donkeys, which had been so badly mistreated by previous owners, but are now being well looked after, living out their lives in comfort.

My murderous thoughts about my father had disappeared by now. When I told him about my experiences, I laid it on thick about how I had learned my lesson, and could he possibly support a donkey sanctuary on our estate. I suppose he was feeling guilty about what he had put me through, because he readily agreed, and that's now my mission in life.

IV

The ramblers had been listening spellbound and spontaneously applauded when she finished.

"Thank you Coralie," said Dan. "What an astonishing story! You deserve our respect and admiration for coming out of it with your head held high."

Percy had been kneeling on one of the backing seats and, making everyone jump, bellowed "What I don't understand is how your father managed to put all that together."

Rosalyn added "And force you to undergo such treatment."

"It will all be in the book," replied Coralie, laughing. "And you lot will get a favourable mention."

Dan continued "Well, I'm sure we'll all look forward to that. Meanwhile, we wish you every success with your donkey sanctuary." There were cheers and cries of 'hear, hear'.

Coralie replied "Thank you. You'd all be very welcome to visit some time, perhaps next year, when we've got everything up and running."

"Where's it located," asked Henry.

"In a remote corner of Daddy's estate, not far from Wendover."

"In the Chilterns. Excellent!" said Henry. "Dan, could we include it on one of our trips?"

"And we'll provide free tea and buns," said Coralie.

"That settles it!" exclaimed Dan. "Are you going to join us on our walk today?"

"Afraid not," replied Coralie. "I have lots to do at the sanctuary, so Jenson is collecting me at Taplow. But I'm so grateful to you for putting up with the old me, and listening to my story."

When the train pulled into Taplow Station, in full view was the white Rolls Royce in the car park, and

Jenson was waiting on the platform. He opened the carriage door and helped Coralie down.

Waving and smiling, she called "See you next year at the sanctuary."

When the train had departed, Coralie turned to Jenson and screeched "Jenson, take me home at once!" It was the old Coralie.

The horrified chauffeur stared open-mouthed. Then the former Honourable Concubine laughed, gave Jenson a hug and kissed him on the cheek.

"Home Jenson," she said, taking his arm, "and don't spare the horses. We'll just save the donkeys!"

CHAPTER 7

EDDIE DISGRACES HIMSELF

Sunday 26th August 1962
Brockenhurst and Holmsley

I

Rosalyn grew up in Ringwood, on the edge of the New Forest in Hampshire. Her parents still lived in a beautiful house and grounds on the eastern outskirts of the town.

On hearing that the excursion on August Bank Holiday Sunday was going to nearby Brockenhurst and Holmsley, Rosalyn's mother, Lucinda, suggested that their daughter should invite Eddie to stay the night. Then they could return home on the Monday.

On the outward train, Rosalyn explained to Dan that she and Eddie would leave Party Number One after lunch in Burley and make their own way to Ringwood. She made sure that this was overheard by Tsubrina, who subsequently became untypically subdued, casting resentful glances at Eddie.

The afternoon route followed by Rosalyn and Eddie took them through purple heather to join Miller's Brook. She knew it well from walks with her parents.

After an hour's walking in glorious heathland on a very warm afternoon, Rosalyn said, "There's a really lovely pond up there in the trees, Miller's Pond. It's well hidden and not many people know about it. Let's have a look."

"Have we got time? We mustn't keep your parents waiting."

"Loads. They don't eat till late on Sundays, so there'll be plenty of time to shower and change."

Rosalyn took Eddie's hand and led him along a narrow, rising path beside a stream. It snaked between trees for some 80 yards, then into view came the clear water of a pond, with an island in the middle.

"It's bigger than it looks," said Rosalyn. "It's shaped like a lop-sided figure-of-eight, and continues around the bend there. We can walk all the way round it. Come on."

Halfway round, Rosalyn said, "See this bank, it used to be my favourite place in all the area. My brother and I used to sit with our feet dangling in the water and throw stones to make ripples."

Then Eddie said, "It looks deep enough to swim. It'll be a great way to cool down."

"But you haven't got a costume, have you?"

"Who needs a costume? There's nobody around."

Rosalyn was shocked and asked, "Is this what you do in Australia?"

"It's what my family did. We lived on an isolated farm by a little river in the foothills of the Blue Mountains.

My brothers and I never wore costumes. We called it skinny-dipping. It feels great, you should try it."

"No thanks. There are people who know me around here. I'd never live it down if I was caught.

As Eddie stripped off, Rosalyn said, "I didn't know you had brothers. How many?"

"Two. Fred and George."

"Any sisters?"

"No, just us boys."

"And your parents?"

"They both died in a plane crash five years ago."

"Oh dear, I'm so sorry. What with Stephanie too... " Her voice trailed off.

"Yes, things have been a bit trying. We sold the farm. Steffie had to move back here, so we decided to get married and try our luck here, while Fred and George wanted to stay in Oz."

Rosalyn looked away as Eddie removed his underpants, but stole a quick glance and smiled as he slid into the water.

Shouting from the water, he said "I'll just go once round the island. I'll only be a few minutes."

It actually took seven minutes, as Eddie stopped to explore the little island. But, on returning to the bank, there was no sign of Rosalyn or his clothes.

"Ros," he called. "Where are you?" There was no reply.

"Come on Ros, stop messing about. Give me my clothes."

There came a tinkling laugh. All through the years he had known her, it was the first time Eddie had heard Rosalyn really laugh. She had always seemed rather serious-minded. Despite his predicament, Eddie thought how attractive it sounded.

The laugh had come from his left. Still naked, he walked gingerly in that direction along the narrow , stony path.

"Wait till I tell your parents about this," he chided.

"Then they'll say you're lying and send you to bed with no dinner."

A small, leafy branch flew out of the trees nearby.

"Cover yourself with that!" ordered Rosalyn. Then she came out from behind the trees, dropped Eddie's clothes on the ground and walked away to continue around the pond.

"Follow me when you're decent!" And with another tinkling laugh, she walked on.

II

Tea and scones with jam and cream awaited Rosalyn and Eddie on arrival at her parents' house.

"Gosh, Mrs Kemp," said Eddie. "This is just what the doctor ordered on a day like this."

"I'm sure you've earned it," said Rosalyn's mother. "How far have you walked today?"

"About ten miles," replied Rosalyn.

"Did she take you to Miller's Pond?"

"She did indeed." Eddie hoped this line of enquiry would not delve too deeply.

"When they were little, Rosalyn and Billy, our son, used to strip off and swim there. I don't suppose it's deep enough for adults."

Eddie glanced at Rosalyn, who was trying to suppress a snigger.

"Probably not," he lied.

After tea, Eddie was invited to take a shower first, then while Rosalyn showered, he was taken on a tour around the vast garden by Colonel Kemp, Rosalyn's father.

"You a gardener?" barked the Colonel.

"Afraid not. The apartments Ros and I live in have a communal garden, and that's looked after by a gardener."

"Pity. We've a gardener too, comes in once a week to do the heavy stuff. But Millicent and I enjoy pottering, planting and trimming and all that sort of thing. Nothing like it for peace of mind. What's the word?"

224

"Therapeutic?" suggested Eddie.

"That's it, well done. Millicent does the flowers, I do the fruit and veg. See those runner beans, and the peas, and the redcurrant bushes. Tomatoes in the greenhouse. All my own work, my pride and joy. Much of this evening's dinner grown by me."

They sat down to dinner at eight o'clock. Despite the tea and scones not so long ago, Eddie still had a voracious appetite and, while the others conversed, cleared his plate in silence. Then he picked up the plate and licked it clean.

"Eddie! What are you doing?" scolded Rosalyn, once again shocked by his behaviour. Her parents watched in amazement.

"Oh, I'm so sorry. What must you think of me?" said an abashed Eddie. "It's just that, back home, we always licked our plates clean to show how much we appreciated Mum's cooking. And I enjoyed Mrs Kemp's cooking and the Colonel's vegetables so much, I just got carried away."

Mrs Kemp beamed and said to Rosalyn and the Colonel, "Well, what are we waiting for?"

As one, all three picked up their plates and licked them clean. The dessert plates, likewise. Then came cheese and biscuits, and liqueurs.

Afterwards, while Eddie and Colonel Kemp discussed cricket and rugby, sipping port in the lounge, Rosalyn helped her mother with the washing-up.

"Eddie certainly has a good appetite," said Mrs Kemp, laughing.

"I don't think he eats very well at home," replied Rosalyn. "He works so hard and long hours."

"Couldn't you… " She was going to say "… cook him something", but Rosalyn knew what was in her mother's mind and frowned. Both were well aware of the younger woman's lack of culinary skill.

"No I couldn't!" she snapped.

After their sumptuous meal, Rosalyn and Eddie slept soundly that night – in separate bedrooms, of course.

III

Eddie stood in the dock.

"The court will rise," called the usher, Dan.

The door at the back of the courtroom opened, and in floated Eddie's late wife, Stephanie. She drifted to the raised high chair behind the bench and sank down onto it.

"Well, Eddie my boy," she said. "You're getting into it deep now, aren't you?"

"I'm confused, your honour."

"Don't speak until you're invited to by the learned gentlewomen," snapped Stephanie.

"Well, you asked a question,"

"Silence in court," shouted Dan.

"Who is prosecuting?" asked Stephanie.

"I am your honour," said a bewigged Tsubrina.

"And who is defending?"

"I am, your honour," said Rosalyn, likewise attired.

"And what is the charge?"

"Bigamy, your honour," yelled Tsubrina. "He's a rat, a dirty rotten cad. I married him first, so he's mine."

"No you didn't," screamed Rosalyn.

The two barristers lunged at each other, ripping each other's gown to shreds.

"Actually," said Stephanie quietly, "I married him first."

Colonel Kemp ran into the courtroom, carrying a rake.

"Leave my daughter alone!" he shouted, and hooked off Tsubrina's wig with the rake.

Luke ran in, bearing a pitchfork, and hooked off Rosalyn's wig. "And you leave my daughter alone!"

Stephanie floated over to Eddie. "Now see what you've done, Eddie my boy. What are you going to do about it?"

"Help me, Steffie! I'm fond of Rosalyn and I fancy Tsubrina. But most of all, I love you. I miss you."

In the customary preparation for a sentence of death, Stephanie put on a black cap.

"May God have mercy on your soul," she said.

"I'm innocent," he yelled.

Stephanie, Rosalyn and Tsubrina all advanced threateningly towards him, then each held out a cup and saucer.

"Here's your early morning tea, sir," they chanted in unison.

Eddie awoke, to find Rosalyn standing next to the bed, carrying a cup and saucer.

"Here's your early morning tea, sir," she said.

CHAPTER 8

THE FAT LADY SINGS

Sunday 9th September 1962
Canterbury East and Shepherds Well

I

Rose's Railway Rambles had so far been quite lucky with the weather in its first season, with just light rain a couple of times, but the forecast for today was 'likelihood of very heavy rain, thunderstorms possible'. Despite which, the morning walk from Shepherds Well had been in bright sunshine, and Party Number One had partaken fully of the ripe blackberries in the hedgerows.

But soon after they left the lunch pub, dark clouds rolled over the horizon and within half an hour had filled the sky. A particularly ominous cumulo-nimbus was approaching from the south, and Henry advised his party to have their waterproofs handy.

Rosalyn was walking at the back, chatting to Peggy, and the subject of laundry arose. As they passed Percy, who had stopped to tie a boot-lace, Peggy said, "Have you tried Spruso, that new washing powder?"

"Not yet," replied Rosalyn. "I've seen it advertised on the telly. Is it any good?"

"Well, it worked well on whites, but I got the distinct impression that the coloureds had faded. They claim it's good for both, so I'm disappointed, especially as it's more expensive than my usual."

"Don't think I'll bother with it, then," said Rosalyn. "I liked the commercial, though. I must admit, some of them are very catchy."

"Oh yes," agreed Peggy. "I love that one about eggs with Tony Hancock."

"And 'The Esso sign means happy motoring', sang Rosalyn, to the toreador tune from 'Carmen'.

"You'll look a little lovelier each day, with fabulous pink Camay," sang Peggy.

"Don't forget the fruit gums, Mum!" added Rosalyn.

Unnoticed by the two women, Percy had caught up and was now right behind them.

"My underpants have turned brown," he blared, so loudly that the whole party turned round to stare, gape and snigger.

"I don't think we want to know that, Percy," said Rosalyn.

"Was it something you had for lunch?" asked Peggy.

"I'm talking about washing powder," droned Percy. "My pants were black when I bought them, but they've gradually turned brown over the years. I suppose all the washing has gradually taken the black dye out."

"Oh, I see," said Rosalyn. "We've moved on from that subject, actually, but anyway, how long have you had them?"

"Oh, I don't know. About six or seven years."

"*S*even years!" exclaimed Peggy. "You should be ashamed of yourself. I buy new ones for Henry every Christmas... amongst other things, of course."

Rosalyn said, "Black underpants indeed. That's a bit racy for you, isn't it? I thought most men wore white underwear."

"I bought them in Paris," said Percy. Which he felt was a satisfactory explanation. Then he added, "I bought some more when I was there a few weeks ago. I'm wearing a pair now."

"Too much information!" exclaimed Peggy.

There was a distant rumble of thunder, and Percy wailed, "Oh dear, I suppose we'll all be killed by lightning now."

"You are a pessimist," laughed Peggy. "I read only the other day that the chances of being struck by lightning are tiny."

"Not with my luck," groaned Percy.

Rosalyn said, "Must say I'm not at all keen on walking in a thunderstorm either."

"Nonsense," protested Peggy. "I think lightning is exciting and beautiful."

Then a flash of lightning was followed a second later by an ear-splitting crack of thunder. Everybody jumped, shouted or screamed, and Percy fell over.

"Bugger!" he yelled.

Then the rain suddenly came down like Noah's flood, and everyone stopped to hastily don their waterproofs.

Henry said, "There's a church hall just ahead, at Mussenden. We can shelter in its porch till this blows over."

Another flash of lightning was accompanied by an almost simultaneous and deafening crack of thunder.

Henry shouted, "Oh my goodness! This is a bit close for comfort. Run, everyone!".

II

The packaging magnate, Sir Peregrine Hobart-Gobb, baronet, had recently moved into Mussenden Hall, together with his wife, Lady

Constance. She had been well known on the operatic stage during the 1930s and 40s as Connie Falwasser, her maiden name. Comic opera, *opera buffa*, and operetta were her specialities, and her sense of humour had endeared her to audiences and opera companies alike.

Now retired, Connie's figure had succumbed to the temptations of gourmet dining and fine wine, and her sight and hearing were sadly deteriorating, but the voice was still in good shape. A kindly soul, soon after her arrival in Mussenden, she had suggested to the vicar of St Ermintrude's, the Reverend Ernest Sherwood, that she should give a free recital of Schubert *lieder* to the parishioners one Sunday afternoon.

The Rev Sherwood privately thought that his flock probably had no idea who Schubert was, let alone any knowledge of his songs. They would more likely appreciate songs from the musicals, or the ribald army songs that old Major Burbot insisted on treating the locals to, late of a Saturday night at the Blacksmith's Arms. But it would have been impolite to decline her ladyship's kind offer.

As the vicar would be preparing his sermon, the task of organising the recital fell to his wife, Ivy. She shared her husband's opinion, and felt that the good people of Mussenden would only turn out for such entertainment if there were other induce-ments. So it was agreed that the church funds could stretch, if necessary, to providing free refreshments, including a glass of wine.

However, this proved to be unnecessary, as the church organist, Miss Aveline Marbles, was locally famous for, and very proud of, her culinary skills — her upside-down cake had won prizes at the Kent County Show — and she willingly agreed to provide, at no cost to the church, a selection of her delicious cakes and pastries.

Then Major Burbot very kindly offered to donate bottles of red and white wine from his extensive cellar. Surely, thought Ivy, all this would bring people out.

The recital was to take place this very day at 3 pm. Mrs Sherwood and Miss Marbles had arrived at the church hall at two o'clock and were busy preparing the refreshments.

Miss Marbles said, "It's turned awfully cold in here, Mrs Sherwood. Should we turn on the heating?"

The vicar's wife looked at the clock on the wall — it was now nearly half past two. "It may be a bit late now," she said. "It takes a good hour to warm the place up, but you're right, it is rather chilly. I'll turn it on."

The hall had recently been fitted with central heating, and just as the vicar's wife was turning it on, a deafening crack of thunder made her jump. Instead of turning the control to halfway, as intended, her hand jolted to full on, and she heard a scream, followed the by the sound of breaking crockery. She rushed into the hall and found Miss Marbles on her knees by the refreshment tables.

"Aveline! Are you all right?"

Miss Marbles looked up. "Oh, Mrs Sherwood, I'm so sorry. It made me jump so much I dropped a plate of upside-down cake onto the table, and would you believe it, it landed upside down. Look, it's ruined!" She was on the verge of tears. Then a second great thunderclap made them both duck, as if the lightning would come in through the door.

The vicar's wife patted Miss Marbles on the shoulder and said, "Never mind, dear. The table's clean, so your lovely cake will still be edible. We'll cut it into slices and nobody will notice. And now we can call it down-side-up cake! It'll be fine. Now where's Major Burbot with the wine?"

Ivy went to the entrance door and looked out. "Oh, just look at this rain! It's coming down in stair-rods. Nobody will come in this. It'll be so embarrassing." She uttered a small prayer to herself, asking the Good Lord to intervene and send an audience.

A black Bentley S2 limousine pulled up in the car park. The chauffeur got out, went round to the passenger side, opened the door, put up an umbrella and escorted Lady Constance Hobart-Gobb into the church hall.

"Good afternoon, Mrs Sherwood," said her ladyship, cheerfully. "But it isn't a very good one, really, is it?"

"Good afternoon, Lady Constance. It's absolutely dreadful. I'm so afraid it's going to keep people away. There's only Miss Marbles, your accompanist, and myself here so far."

"I'm afraid you'll have to speak up. I'm a little deaf."

Mrs Sherwood repeated the gist of her statement, *forte*.

Lady Constance looked blank. "No, sorry, not catching it. My husband keeps telling me to get a hearing aid, but I can't stand the wretched things. They start whistling when you least expect it. Have another go!"

The vicar's wife tried again, *fortissimo*.

"Got it this time, well done. Nobody here, eh? Can't say I blame 'em, in this weather. Never mind, happy to sing just for you, if necessary."

"Well, there's Miss Marbles as well," yelled Mrs Sherwood. "She'll be accompanying you on the piano."

"Miss Marple, did you say? Isn't she a detective?"

"Marbles."

"Two of 'em?"

236

Mrs Sherwood gave up, led Lady Constance into the hall and introduced her to Miss Marbles.

"Delighted to meet you," said her ladyship. "Are you investigating another murder?"

Miss Marbles looked quizzically at Mrs Sherwood, who raised her eyebrows and shouted, "Would you care for some tea and cake, Lady Constance?"

"Goodness me, what a wonderful spread! Just tea, please. I'll leave the cake until after I've sung. But who's prepared all this food?"

"Miss Marbles made it," yelled Ivy. "She's a wonderful cook."

"What a treasure!" exclaimed her Ladyship. "Not just a brilliant detective and pianist but a gourmet chef as well."

As Miss Marbles poured the tea, Mrs Sherwood said, "I'll just go and see if anyone's coming."

III

Party Number One, led by Henry, ran down the lane and reached the gate of Mussenden's church hall. then fought each other to get into the porch.

Mrs Sherwood watched them, looked skywards and muttered, "Thank you, Lord!"

Henry counted his charges. There were fourteen, but there should have been fifteen.

"Where's Percy?" he called.

"Been struck by lightning, I expect," answered Peggy, brightly.

"Oh, don't!" exclaimed Rosalyn. "That'd be tragic in view of his earlier remark."

The wind was driving the rain onto the porch. The vicar's wife said to Henry, "You'd better come inside. We're having a recital and you're most welcome to stay. It's about to start, and it's free."

Henry said, "That's very kind of you, but we've got to get to Canterbury. It's five miles."

"Don't worry about that," said Dan. Bekesbourne station is just over a mile away, so we can return from there. Might be best to cut it short, anyway, in this weather."

"And there's free tea, wine and cakes," added Mrs Sherwood.

"That settles it then," said Peggy, to a general murmur of approval. "But we're all soaked. We'll drip water all over your chairs."

"Oh," Ivy looked concerned for a moment, then brightened and said "I know! If you go through the door beside the stage, you'll see some wardrobes at the back. They're full of costumes for our Christmas pantomimes. You can put your wet things on the radiators and wear the costumes while they dry."

There was some consternation amongst the ramblers at this, but they entered into the spirit and did as they were bidden.

Dan said, "I'd better go and look for Percy. He's still outside somewhere.

But then Percy staggered in, dripping wet. "Couldn't get my poncho out of the rucksack," he bawled. "Soaked through." His long khaki shorts, which usually reached just below the knees, had now stretched to below his calves, while black dye from his underpants ran down his legs.

The ramblers trooped off and returned some minutes later, amid much laughter, wearing an assortment of colourful outfits – most outrageously Percy, whose shorts had been replaced by the front legs of a pantomime horse, while the head dangled loose in front. "They're the only things that would fit," he moaned.

The main door opened to reveal a tall, burly man with a florid complexion and a handlebar moustache, covered by a great cape and a broad-brimmed hat. He was carrying a box that was clearly heavy.

"At last," cried Ivy. "Here's Major Burbot with the wine."

"Sorry I'm late," rasped the Major, his voice betraying years of heavy drinking and cigar-smoking. "Thought I'd wait till the rain stopped, but it hasn't, and I couldn't wait any longer. Didn't want to let you down, Ivy."

"Thanks ever so much. So good of you to donate the wine. Are you wet?"

"No, this army cape won't let anything through. But what's going on? Who are these people and why are they wearing those ridiculous outfits?"

Ivy explained, then the Major said, "Well, that's a bit of a blessing, then. I was rather hoping…er, afraid nobody would turn up, then more wine for us, what!"

"The Good Lord has provided, Major," said Ivy. "They're ramblers. Or perhaps I should say pilgrims, and we're honoured to provide them with sustenance and entertainment to help them on their journey to salvation."

Eddie, standing behind Ivy, winced at this remark and whispered to Rosalyn, "Oh dear! In that case it'll be wasted on me."

Rosalyn looked at him in surprise and said, "Does that mean you're a non-believer?"

"Yes. Are you offended?"

"Well yes, I am a bit."

"I'm sorry then. But I'd have thought that most people who go rambling on Sundays have no real faith, otherwise they'd be in church."

"Just because they don't go to church doesn't mean they don't believe in God. I say my prayers every day, for good health and happiness for all my friends... including you!" There was a hint of resentment in Rosalyn's voice.

Eddie looked at the floor, then looked up and said, "Well, I'm very grateful. I sincerely wish all my friends good health and happiness too, but I don't think praying for it would make the slightest difference. We'd better leave it there."

They were silent for a moment, then Rosalyn said, "Let's get something to eat, those cakes look delicious."

Ivy Sherwood went to the piano by the stage and clapped her hands. "Silence please. I hope you've all refreshed yourselves. May I please ask you to take your seats now, as Lady Constance is very kindly going to entertain us with some *lieder* – songs by Franz Schubert. We are indeed honoured as she is better known as Connie Falwasser, who toured the world in many operatic roles."

There was an audible gasp and some muttering, as some of the ramblers had heard of her.

"Connie – she's happy to be called that – will start with one of my favourites, and I hope one of yours too. *'Die Forelle'*, which means 'The Trout'. It's in German, of course, but briefly it tells the story of a man watching an angler trying to catch a trout. At first the water's too clear and the trout evades the hook, but the crafty angler stirs up the mud and the poor creature gets caught in the end, much to the dismay of the spectator, who's on the side of the trout. Now please give Connie a warm welcome."

Major Burbot wound the stage curtains open to reveal Her Ladyship, and the ramblers applauded enthusiastically – a little too enthusiastically on the part of Joaquín, who had already knocked back two glasses of wine – he stuck two fingers in his mouth and produced a piercing whistle.

As Miss Marbles played the introduction, the catch on the winding mechanism broke and the curtains closed.

Lady Constance, now behind the curtains again, laughed and called, "Make up your mind!"

The Major tried again and wedged the winding wheel with a piece of wood. The piano intro was repeated and Connie started to sing:

"In einem Bächlein helle,
Da schoss in froher Eil..."

Since retiring from the stage, Connie had developed a slight tic, in which she jerked her head sideways when drawing breath. She did that now and continued:

"Die launische Forelle

Vorüber wie ein Pfeil...”

Jerk.

Most unfortunately, some of the ramblers found this amusing and started sniggering. The radiators were getting very hot now, and one of them started to knock at regular intervals.

“Ich stand an dem Gestade (knock)
Und sah in süsser Ruh’...” (jerk)

The central heating was now full on, and it had become very warm in the hall. Percy had fallen asleep and started to snore. This set off more sniggering. Mrs Sherwood looked round and put a shushing finger to her lips.

“Des muntern Fischleins Bade (knock, snore)
Im klaren Bächlein zu.” (jerk, snore)

As the first verse came to an end, Peggy nudged Percy, who awoke with a start and yelled “What’s up?” Then somebody farted, very loudly. The combination of head-jerking, radiator-knocking, snoring, Percy’s untimely intervention and now the breaking of wind was overwhelming. Sniggers turned into outright laughter, and the vicar’s wife covered her face with her hands. This was turning into a disaster, but the short-sighted and deaf Connie was oblivious and launched into the second verse:

“Ein Fischer mit der Rute (knock, snore)

Wohl an…"

But before she had a chance to sing "*dem Ufer stand*", there was an almighty flash and simultaneous thunderclap, a direct hit on the church spire – which, fortunately, was fitted with a lightning conductor. The lights went out. Plates, cups and glasses were dropped and smashed on the floor. Miss Marbles screamed and dived under the piano. Percy fell off his chair. Everyone else ducked down between the seats.

Major Burbot's wedge in the winding wheel popped out, the curtains closed over Connie; she lost her balance, and in falling to the ground grabbed hold of a curtain. This dislodged the curtain-rail and the whole assemblage collapsed on top of her, though this went unnoticed by everyone else as they were in hiding, wondering what calamity would come next.

All this took place within a few seconds, then there was an almost total silence, except for the rain, still drumming at the windows.

Dan stood up and called, "Is everyone okay?"

It seemed that they were, but from the stage came the sound of muffled laughter. It was Connie, under the curtains.

The vicar's wife was horrified. "Oh, goodness, Lady Constance. Quick, someone, help her!"

Dan, Eddie, Henry, and naturally Joaquín, rushed forward, untangled the curtains and helped the still laughing ladyship to her feet.

"What fun," she said. "I haven't had so much excitement since the stage lift at the Opéra-Comique in Paris accidentally propelled me skywards in the middle of 'Mio Babbino Caro'."

Mrs Sherwood said to Miss Marbles, "Aveline, would you please turn the urn back on, we all need a nice cup of tea to revive ourselves. Come on everyone, there's plenty of cake and wine left. I want it all finished before you go."

And finish it all off they did. Not a slice of cake, not a drop of wine, was left. Lady Constance sang a few Gilbert and Sullivan songs, though somewhat below her usual standard, due to the cake she had consumed. Major Burbot started to sing one of his ribald army songs, but was hastily shushed by Mrs Sherwood after the first verse.

Lady Constance led a conga around the hall, with the ramblers still in their pantomime costumes. Then, as the rain had stopped, they congaed around the graveyard. Connie was about to take it into the church itself, but the Reverend Sherwood, arriving to prepare for Benediction, strongly opposed the notion. Seeing his wife near the back of the line, he severely reprimanded her for allowing such unseemly behaviour.

"Don't be such a spoilsport, Ernest," she retorted. "Come along, join in!"

The Reverend Sherwood, shocked, stood agape. Then he shrugged, laughed and tagged on at the end.

CHAPTER 9

SEAFORD HEAD

Sunday 23rd September 1962
Berwick and Seaford

I

The promise of fine weather, and the wonderful walking territory served by today's destinations, had resulted in a record turnout for Rose's Railway Rambles, especially as it was the last of the summer programme.

The loyal followers of Henry and Peggy, and of Luke and Tsubrina, were all there, plus Muttley's Marchers, the Mudlarks and the Happy Wanderers, as well as half a dozen complete newcomers. A grand total of sixty-two occupied the front two coaches of the Eastbourne train, which would make a special stop at Berwick for the ramblers' benefit.

Dan was feeling rather pleased with himself. He thought the first season had gone well, all things considered.

Tsubrina was not so happy. Although she enjoyed the attentions of the men who regularly joined Party Number Two, she found them boring. Furthermore, Eddie seemed to be getting ever more closely involved with Rosalyn, and that hurt.

Rosalyn and Eddie, too, seemed discontented. They maintained a gloomy silence for the whole journey, only speaking when they were spoken to by others. The reason for this was a dispute on the way to Victoria Station about a proposal by the management of their apartments to build a children's playground in the communal garden. Rosalyn was for, Eddie against.

Furthermore, it had emerged during this altercation that, while Rosalyn hoped to start a family in due course, Eddie had no interest in doing so. Indeed, his late wife, Stephanie, had been unable to have children, and neither of them was particularly bothered about it.

Having got to know Eddie better recently, Rosalyn was having doubts about their compatability. So when Eddie announced that he would be joining Party Number Two this time, Tsubrina brightened up considerably, while Rosalyn just said "Huh!" and remained tight-lipped for the rest of the journey.

The reason Eddie gave for this was that Party Number Two would make Alfriston their lunch stop, while Party Number One went to Litlington. He had heard what an attractive village Alfriston was, and would like to see it, but Rosalyn was not convinced. Clearly, she thought, he just preferred to be with Tsubrina.

The routes of all the ramblers would converge at Exceat Bridge. Dan had made arrangements with the Golden Galleon pub there, to provide a grand end-of-season tea for everyone, then they would all walk together past Cuckmere Haven and over Seaford Head to finish at Seaford.

During the outward journey, the ramblers engaged in a heated discussion about the pronunciation of place names. Alf-riston or Orl-friston? Should Cuckmere be pronounced Cookmere? Eck-set or Eck-seat? Dan said he didn't know any other area where there was so much disagreement about the matter. Normally, Rosalyn would have been an eager participant in this subject, but today she just stared glumly out of the window.

But for everyone else, everything looked good for a perfect day: delightful walking in gorgeous scenery; excellent pubs; bright sunshine, quite warm, but with a brisk onshore breeze bringing cooler air off the English Channel and up the Cuckmere Valley. However, things started badly, and were to get much worse.

II

Let us start with Party Number One. Their route first went eastwards from Berwick Station.

At a junction, Henry said, "We turn right here, but Arlington Reservoir's just two hundred yards to the left. So we'll go and have a quick look at it."

On reaching the reservoir, Hitomi, the Japanese woman, said, "Please, I take photograph of you. Will you please line up along the wall."

249

The ramblers did as asked, and Hitomi took several snaps with the reservoir in the background. Then she said, "I think I will also take one from the water looking up."

As she clambered down the sloping bank, Peggy called, "Do be careful, it could be slippery there."

But Hitomi had already lost her footing and slid, rather gracefully, into the water, though she had the presence of mind to throw her camera up to the grassy top.

"Oh, no!" said everyone, almost in unison.

"Help! I cannot swim," she cried.

Joaquín theatrically placed his hand on his chest, shouted, "I, Joaquín Carlos Roca Diaz, will save you!"

Then he bowed to the line of ramblers and ran down the slope. But he too slipped and slid into the water.

"'Elp, I cannot swim," he cried.

Dan and Henry started down the slope, and Peggy yelled, "Now don't you go falling in!" But slip and slide into the water they did.

"You idiots!" shouted Peggy. Don't anyone else go down or we'll all end up in there."

Dan and Henry had got hold of Hitomi and Joaquín, keeping their heads above water, but every time they tried to climb the slippery bank, they slid back in.

Rosalyn said, "There's a lifebelt along there. I'll get it."

She ran the hundred yards to the lifebelt and returned with it, but said, "This is no use. There's no rope attached. How are we going to pull them out?"

"This is a disaster," said Peggy. "Look, there's a building over there. We'd better try for help there."

Rosalyn ran to the building, which was a farmhouse, found a man about to climb into a tractor and explained the situation.

"Oh no, not again!" he exclaimed. "I keep tellin' em to put a fence around, but they won't listen. Just a moment, I'll get a rope."

As they pulled out the four sodden ramblers, Peggy said, "Just as well it's a warm day. You should be reasonably dry by the time we get to Litlington."

A very embarrassed Hitomi bowed deeply and said, "I am so sorry for the trouble I have caused. Please forgive me."

"Never mind," said Dan. "I expect we'll all be laughing about it on the way home." But he was wrong.

II

Now we turn to Party Number Two, heading west at first. Soon after starting, by a farmhouse just half a mile from Berwick Station, the party passed an elderberry tree. Up a ladder, obscured by trailing branches, was the farmer's wife, collecting berries.

Luke Trayton, Tsubrina's father, in the lead, spotted the ladder and warned the followers. However,

251

Eddie, near the back, engaged in conversation with Tsubrina, failed to hear the warning and walked straight into the ladder. The farmer's wife fell onto Eddie, he fell onto Tsubrina and the basket, now full of elderberries, landed upside-down on Tsubrina's head.

"Strewth, I'm so sorry. What a drongo!" exclaimed Eddie. "Are you both alright?" But the two women just glared at him.

He went to remove the basket from Tsubrina's head, then saw what looked like blood trickling down her face.

"Oh my, Tsubrina, you've been cut!" he exclaimed, then shouted, "Luke! Tsubrina's hurt. Do you have a first aid kit?"

As a former army sergeant, for all his faults, Luke did come well prepared. He knelt down beside his daughter, took out the kit, then looked closely at her face.

"This doesn't look like blood," he said, then dabbed his finger on the liquid, tasted it and laughed. "It's only bloody elderberry juice!"

"Of course it's elderberry juice," said the farmer's wife. "That's because the basket was full of elderberries." She removed the basket from Tsubrina's head. "Now look at them!"

"They'll be alright," said Luke. "You can't eat elderberries just like that anyway. You have to crush them and add sugar to make something edible, like wine or jam."

"I know that," laughed the farmer's wife. "I was only teasing." She took the basket, re-erected the ladder and continued picking.

As Party Number Two resumed their ramble, Eddie helped Tsubrina up, then laughed.

"What's so funny?" she asked.

Eddie laughed and said, "Your hair is streaked pink. You look like a hippy."

Tsubrina pouted. "It's not funny!"

But Eddie said, "Actually, it's rather attractive. You should keep it like that."

The pout disintegrated into a broad grin. "Thank you. Maybe I will."

She put her arms around his neck and kissed him on the lips. At first, Eddie was minded to resist, but found he was enjoying it, and the kiss went on for a rather long time. Then Tsubrina laughed, took Eddie's hand, and they ran to catch up.

Their lunch stop, the Smugglers Inn at Alfriston, was under new management. The landlord had pre-tentions of making this historic inn a gastronomic magnet for the local gentry. Previously welcoming to all and sundry, including ramblers, a sign had been placed by the door: "No muddy boots and no rucksacks inside". Muddy boots, understandable, but rucksacks?

Boots were not muddy anyway in the current dry weather, but Luke ignored the rucksack ban, dropped his in the fireplace, then went to order his drink at the bar.

On seeing the offending item, the landlord yelled, "Who put that rucksack there?"

Luke laughed and quipped "It fell down the chimney!"

"Right!" exclaimed mine host. "Stop serving them. Get out, all of you!"

And so Party Number Two somewhat shamefacedly made their way along the High Street to continue their lunch break in the George, where rucksacks were tolerated.

III

Party Number One's lunch stop at Litlington had been rather muted. Several members were still quite damp after their soaking, but dried off a little while sitting in the sunny garden.

As planned, everyone came together for tea in the garden of the Golden Galleon at Exceat Bridge. Both the official parties, as well as the Happy Wanderers and the Mudlarks, were there. Even Muttley's Marchers had called a halt to their usual incessant marching and sat down.

Seeing as this was the last Rose's Railway Ramble of the season, most of the ramblers had imbibed rather freely at the lunch pubs. Normally, pubs had to close on Sunday afternoons, but the landlord of the Golden Galleon had obtained a special licence to serve alcohol with the afternoon tea. It seemed too good an opportunity to miss, but was to turn out a bad decision

Everyone was in celebratory, end-of-season mood, having consumed rather too much alcohol at lunchtime. Even the normally sober Rosalyn, drowning her sorrows, had downed a pint of rather strong cider, and now unwisely decided to have a glass of white wine with her afternoon tea.

Eddie and Tsubrina were sat at the next table, with their backs towards Rosalyn. Taking a scone, she hurled it towards Tsubrina, hitting her squarely on the back of the head, whence it fell to the floor.

Tsubrina turned, saw Rosalyn and correctly guessed the source of the missile. Taking a bread roll, she threw it hard towards Rosalyn, but her aim was not so good, and it hit Percy instead.

"Who threw that?" enquired Percy. Not receiving an answer, he felt obliged to get revenge anyway, and threw the bread roll in the air, not caring where it might land. The destination proved to be Peggy's cup of tea, whose contents splashed over the tablecloth.

Peggy removed the soggy roll and likewise tossed it in the air. It landed on Pochette Saucy's head. The Mudlarks thought this was great fun, and began hurling bread rolls and sugar cubes at all and sundry. Soon everyone was at it. Cups and jugs of milk were knocked over. A waiter tried to intervene, but for his trouble received a complete, unsliced coffee-and-walnut cake on his head.

The landlord came out and yelled, "Stop this immediately!" And to Dan he said, "So Mr Rose, explain yourself. You'll have to pay for all this damage and the cleaning."

Eventually, order was restored. Dan apologised profusely, and said he would pay whatever the landlord felt was a fair price. The ramblers were told to get out – for the second time that day in the case of Party Number Two.

Down in the car park, Peggy called everyone together and said, "I'm ashamed of myself. Not like me at all, or most of us I guess. We should all be ashamed of ourselves." This was met by murmurs of agreement.

"Dan, we humbly apologise," she continued. "We'll have a collection to cover what you've had to pay."

Dan said nothing, just nodded, and set off along the track towards Cuckmere Haven, followed by a long line of silent ramblers.

IV

Conversation gradually resumed on the long climb from Hope Gap to Seaford Head. Dan had warned everyone to keep well away from the cliff edge, as it was notoriously unstable. Once upon a time, the land had extended all the way to France, but thousands of years ago, it is thought, an awesome tsunami started

256

a process that created the English Channel, turning Britain into an island. To this day, the combined action of storms, waves and ice knock great chunks of chalk off the white cliffs every year.

Despite warning notices, there are always foolhardy people who venture too close to the cliff edge, curious to see what lies below. Tsubrina succumbed to the temptation.

There was a sudden loud crack and the ground she was on started to slip away. After a few nail-biting seconds, it came to a halt, five feet below the top. Tsubrina, who was not much taller, had almost disappeared, but then her blonde hair appeared over the cliff edge.

Luke and Dan, who were nearest, ran over and held out their hands for Tsubrina to grab and started to haul her up.

"My foot's stuck," she cried.

Eddie shouted, "Keep hold of her," and lowered himself gently beside Tsubrina.

"No Eddie, please don't!" shouted Rosalyn.

But Eddie was already beside Tsubrina, and managed to free her foot. She was hauled up, but just as Eddie went to lift himself up, there was a thunderous roar, and the whole slab crashed down, taking Eddie with it.

V

Stephanie hovered over Eddie in a golden glow.

"That was a bit drastic, wasn't it? You didn't have to do that."

"I only want to be with you, Steffie."

"You silly boy, you had so much to live for."

"I tried. I tried really hard, but I couldn't live without you."

Stephanie sighed, held out a hand and said, "All right, come with me then."

CHAPTER 10

EPILOGUE

Friday 12th October 1962
St Mary's, Islington

I

Eddie's funeral took place at St Mary's Church in Highbury, near the apartments where he and Rosalyn lived. It was well attended, as Eddie had become a popular fixture on the ramblers' excursions. All the regulars from Parties Numbers One and Two were there, as well as the Happy Wanderers and the Mudlarks. The funeral was due to take place at 11 a.m., and they had started to gather outside the entrance earlier, suitably attired for a funeral and engaged in muted conversation.

Luke and Tsubrina, though, were not among them.

Winnie expressed the thoughts of many present. "She wouldn't dare show her face, after what happened."

"That's not fair," said Dan. "Eddie didn't have to do what he did. We could have found another way of freeing her."

Rosalyn said nothing. For nearly two weeks, uppermost in her thoughts was the knowledge that she, too, had been instrumental in bringing about

Eddie's demise, by persuading him to come on the rambles.

The vicar came up to her. "How are you?" he enquired.

"Bearing up," she replied, though she could not suppress a tear.

The vicar patted her shoulder. "I'm sure you'll be fine," he said. "Ah, here's the hearse."

The long, black vehicle pulled up to the church door and the funeral director alighted, together with four assistants. There was no cortège as there was no family of the deceased present.

The director approached Rosalyn. "I'm so sorry, Miss Kemp. We cabled the funeral details to Mr Leaney's brothers, but no response I'm afraid."

"Oh dear. I would so like to have met his brothers,"

Rosalyn had tried very hard to contact them. She had been allowed into his apartment and found Fred's address, to which she had sent two telegrams, with no answer. The telephone number shown was a ceased line. The funeral director had offered to help, with the same result. She had also asked for assistance from the Australian High Commission, but they too had failed to make contact, and gave permission for the funeral to take place.

The funeral director said, "Well, as there's apparently no family present, if you have no objection, may I suggest that you and Mr Leaney's closest friends take up the front row on the left?"

The bearers pulled the coffin from the hearse and carried it into the church, led by the director.

After a few minutes, the vicar turned to the mourners and said, "Would you please follow me inside. As there's no family, you may sit either side. But please fill the rows from the front backwards."

Then a taxi pulled up, the door opened and Luke got out. He was sombrely dressed, but had no tie.

Dan said, "You really ought to wear a tie at a funeral, Luke."

"Got one in my pocket, I'll put it on before I go in. Can't stand ties. Stupid things."

Where's Tsubrina?" asked Dan.

"Paying the driver. She'll be out in a minute."

The woman who emerged was hardly recognisable. She wore a black, loose-fitting jacket, which hid the notorious amplitude of her bosom, a black skirt that came to just below the knees, and black, low-heeled Oxford shoes. Her blonde hair had been cut very short, and on top of it was a black pillbox hat. A pair of dark glasses covered her eyes.

"I don't believe it," whispered Henry. "It's Tsubrina!"

The ramblers stood aghast. It was the first time any of the ramblers had seen her dressed demurely.

Tsubrina walked up to Rosalyn and removed the glasses. She started to say something, but the words would not come. Rosalyn, too, was unable to speak. She saw how haggard the younger woman looked, betraying many sleepless nights. For the first time, both women felt a common bond.

Rosalyn led the regulars of Party Number One into the front left-hand row: Winnie, Dan, Peggy, Henry, Percy, Joaquín and Hitomi. Oliver sat with Dan.

Tsubrina, Luke and the regulars from Party Number Two, including Preston Twite, Horace Gravey (who wore his usual clothes) and the Scotsman (still wearing his tartan jacket), filed into the front two right-hand rows. The Happy Wanderers took the second row on the left, and the Mudlarks the third row on the right.

The organist was quietly playing the traditional hymn, "We shall Walk Through the Valley in Peace". But it was accompanied by a regular thump, which seemed out of place. Then, in the background, could be heard "Left, right, left right... " It was Muttley's Marchers.

The Major at least had the courtesy to stop shouting as they entered the church and removed their forage caps, but continued marching in single file along the aisle, with the little one trying to keep up at the back.

On reaching the third row on the left, Muttley whispered loudly "Left turn!" Then, on reaching its end, "Halt!" They halted. And "Sit!" They sat.

The funeral director closed the door, and the vicar turned to the congregation.

"We are gathered here today …" he began.

Then the door burst open, everyone turned, and in came… Eddie!

Tsubrina screamed. Rosalyn said, "Oooh!" Then they both fainted, and everyone else gaped in amazement.

Henry said, "Talk about being late for your own funeral!"

Then in came … another Eddie!

"Sorry we're late," said the first Eddie.

There was pandemonium, everyone talking at once.

II

Rosalyn and Tsubrina were brought round with smelling salts. The vicar invited the Eddies to come to the front and explain themselves.

One Eddie said, "Gosh, folks, I'm really sorry we've caused such a fuss. We thought you knew. We were triplets. I'm Fred, and this is George."

Rosalyn said, weakly, "Eddie told me he had two brothers but didn't say you were triplets."

Order was restored. Room was found in the front left row for Fred and George, and the service continued.

Afterwards, outside the church, Dan announced that there was to be a reception in the King's Head pub opposite.

Fred and George were the centre of attention. Everyone gathered round and plied them with questions. The brothers, too, had many questions to ask about Eddie.

Rosalyn asked "Why didn't you reply to our telegrams?"

"We were on holiday," replied Fred, "and out of contact, sailing a yacht around the Solomon Islands."

"We didn't get home until Friday," continued George, "then it was such a shock, and an almighty rush, booking a flight and sorting things out. We were supposed to be back at work yesterday."

Fred added "It's all been a bit of a strain lately. We both got divorced earlier this year. We're still on good terms with our wives, but they have custody of the children. That's why we took the sailing trip, to get over the stress. But now this!"

Dan called "Come on everyone, give them some space. I'm sure they would like time to reflect at this sad time."

Fred said, "It's okay. Of course it's sad, but we had time on the plane to discuss what we want to do.

George continued, "Some of you may know that Eddie ran a travel business here. Well, we work for a big travel agency back in Oz. They've been considering opening a London branch for some time, and asked us to find out if it might be possible to take over Eddie's business for that."

Fred took over. "So George will stay here for a while to check it out. I fly home tomorrow, then if it works out I'll come back here to help him."

"And if you don't mind, Rosalyn," said George, "I'll be using Eddie's apartment for a while, as a base and to sort out his things."

"Oh, no, of course I don't mind," said Rosalyn, rather surprised. "It will be good to have someone occupying it.

Dan said, "Raise your glasses everyone! Here's to Eddie."

"Eddie!" came the response.

Then Henry said, "And here's success to Fred and George!"

"Success to Fred and George!"

Peggy said, "And we hope you'll come walking with us."

But Dan interrupted. "Before you get carried away, I'm not sure I'll continue with Rose's Railway Rambles after what happened at Seaford Head. I've rather lost heart."

"Don't' be silly, Dan," said Peggy, "Sure, it was tragic, but we've had such a great time otherwise. It would be even more tragic to just let them go."

"I'm sure Eddie would have liked you to keep going," said George. "We used to hike a lot in the Blue Mountains together."

Fred said "He told us what a great time he was having, with you lot, and how wonderful the hiking is over here."

"Well, I'll think it over," said Dan. "I haven't planned anything for the winter, but I'll see how I feel in a month or so and let you all know."

Rosalyn and Tsubrina looked at each other. They were still shocked and confused, but knew what was in the other's mind. Which of the remaining triplets should each of them pursue?

THE END

ABOUT THE AUTHOR

Colin Saunders was born in Barnet in 1942 and spent most of his working life in travel and tourism. He has been self-employed since 1989 as an organiser of walking holidays and events and as a manager of walkers' trails.

He is the author of guides to some of the finest walking routes in London and South East England: the Capital Ring, the London Loop, the North Downs Way national trail, the Pymmes Brook Trail and the Vanguard Way. And together with Slovak mountain guide Renáta Nárožná, their guide to the High Tatras range of Poland and Slovakia is regarded as the definitive English language guide to these beautiful mountains.

Fifty Paces Forward is Colin's first venture into the world of fiction, but he has also written some fascinating historical accounts about walking phenomena:

Rambling Away From 'The Smoke' (about the ramblers' excursions from London);

The Strollerthon Story (a fabulous fundraising event for children's charities);

The Waymark Story (about Waymark Holidays, a small but remarkable operator of walking and cross-country skiing holidays).

Full details at colinsaunders.org.uk.